Doing What's Right . . .

"I can't go look for him, Mr. Adams," Jason said. "I can look after my brother, and my sisters, but I know I'm too small, too young to go and find him. So I been saving money until I could find somebody to go and find him for us."

"And that's me?"

"I saw what you done yesterday, in front of the saloon," Jason said. "You ain't afraid of nothin'. You can do anythin'."

"You can do it, Mr. Adams," Jenny said. "You got to!"

"We need our pa," Jason said.

"Yes, you do," Clint said. "You do need your father."

"Then you'll do it?" Jenny asked.

"If you'll call me Clint," he said to her, "I'll do it."

"Oh, Clint." She got up, ran around the table, and threw her arms around his neck.

What had he gotten himself into this time?

D0834303

DON'T MISS THESE
ALL-ACTION WESTERN SERIES
FROM THE BERKLEY PUBLISHING GROUP

THE GUNSMITH by J. R. Roberts
Clint Adams was a legend among lawmen, outlaws, and ladies. They called him . . . the Gunsmith.

LONGARM by Tabor Evans
The popular long-running series about Deputy U.S. Marshal Custis Long—his life, his loves, his fight for justice.

SLOCUM by Jake Logan
Today's longest-running action Western. John Slocum rides a deadly trail of hot blood and cold steel.

BUSHWHACKERS by B. J. Lanagan
An action-packed series by the creators of Longarm! The rousing adventures of the most brutal gang of cutthroats ever assembled—Quantrill's Raiders.

DIAMONDBACK by Guy Brewer
Dex Yancey is Diamondback, a Southern gentleman turned con man when his brother cheats him out of the family fortune. Ladies love him. Gamblers hate him. But nobody pulls one over on Dex . . .

WILDGUN by Jack Hanson
The blazing adventures of mountain man Will Barlow—from the creators of Longarm!

TEXAS TRACKER by Tom Calhoun
J.T. Law: the most relentless—and dangerous—manhunter in all Texas. Where sheriffs and posses fail, he's the best man to bring in the most vicious outlaws—for a price.

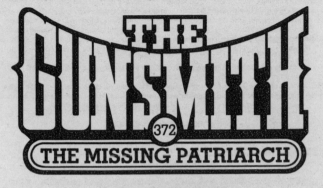

THE GUNSMITH

372

THE MISSING PATRIARCH

J. R. ROBERTS

JOVE BOOKS, NEW YORK

THE BERKLEY PUBLISHING GROUP
Published by the Penguin Group
Penguin Group (USA) Inc.
375 Hudson Street, New York, New York 10014, USA
Penguin Group (Canada), 90 Eglinton Avenue East, Suite 700, Toronto, Ontario M4P 2Y3, Canada
(a division of Pearson Penguin Canada Inc.) • Penguin Books Ltd., 80 Strand, London WC2R 0RL,
England • Penguin Group Ireland, 25 St. Stephen's Green, Dublin 2, Ireland (a division of Penguin
Books Ltd.) • Penguin Group (Australia), 250 Camberwell Road, Camberwell, Victoria 3124, Australia
(a division of Pearson Australia Group Pty. Ltd.) • Penguin Books India Pvt. Ltd., 11 Community
Centre, Panchsheel Park, New Delhi—110 017, India • Penguin Group (NZ), 67 Apollo Drive,
Rosedale, Auckland 0632, New Zealand (a division of Pearson New Zealand Ltd.) • Penguin Books
(South Africa) (Pty.) Ltd., 24 Sturdee Avenue, Rosebank, Johannesburg 2196, South Africa

Penguin Books Ltd., Registered Offices: 80 Strand, London WC2R 0RL, England

This is a work of fiction. Names, characters, places, and incidents either are the product of the author's
imagination or are used fictitiously, and any resemblance to actual persons, living or dead, business
establishments, events, or locales is entirely coincidental.

THE MISSING PATRIARCH

A Jove Book / published by arrangement with the author

PUBLISHING HISTORY
Jove edition / December 2012

Copyright © 2012 by Robert J. Randisi.
Cover illustration by Sergio Giovine.

All rights reserved.
No part of this book may be reproduced, scanned, or distributed in any printed or
electronic form without permission. Please do not participate in or encourage piracy of
copyrighted materials in violation of the author's rights. Purchase only authorized editions.
For information, address: The Berkley Publishing Group,
a division of Penguin Group (USA) Inc.,
375 Hudson Street, New York, New York 10014.

ISBN: 978-0-515-15123-7

JOVE®
Jove Books are published by The Berkley Publishing Group,
a division of Penguin Group (USA) Inc.,
375 Hudson Street, New York, New York 10014.
JOVE® is a registered trademark of Penguin Group (USA) Inc.
The "J" design is a trademark of Penguin Group (USA) Inc.

PRINTED IN THE UNITED STATES OF AMERICA

10 9 8 7 6 5 4 3 2 1

If you purchased this book without a cover, you should be aware that this book is
stolen property. It was reported as "unsold and destroyed" to the publisher, and neither the
author nor the publisher has received any payment for this "stripped book."

ALWAYS LEARNING   **PEARSON**

ONE

Jason McCall entered the house, carrying the meager result of his hunt over his shoulder.

"Rabbit again?" his brother, Simon, complained.

"Be quiet," his sister Jenny said. She took the rabbits from her brother, carried them to the sink. "Your brother is doing the best he can for us."

"Why can't I go out huntin' with him?" Simon complained.

"You'll shoot your foot off," Jason said. "Ain't you supposed to be outside with your sister, helpin' her clean out the barn?"

"Aw, that ain't no job for a man!"

"Well, when you're a man, you can make that decision," Jason said. "Go out and help Jesse."

"Aw, yes, sir."

After Simon left the house, Jason sat down at the table, his shoulders slumped.

"What's wrong?"

"I got to go into town."

"What for?"

"We need some supplies."

"How you gonna buy them?" Jenny asked. "We already owe enough money to Mr. Mason at the mercantile."

"Maybe I can get some more credit from him," Jason said. "Do we have any money?"

Jenny went to the cupboard, opened it, and took down a tin cup. She carried it to the table, dumped out the contents. All coins. Jason counted them.

"A dollar and fifteen cents," he said. "I can probably get somethin' for that."

"We need some flour," she said, "and some milk."

"Okay," Jason said. He stood up, and pocketed the money. "Maybe I can get some hard candy for the kids."

"They don't need candy," she said.

"Yeah, okay."

"Are you takin' the horse?" she asked. "The buckboard?"

"I won't have enough supplies to need the buckboard," he said. "I'll just saddle the horse."

He went to the wall and took down his Winchester.

"Do you really need to take that?"

"I'm goin' to town," he said, as if that was answer enough.

In place of the Winchester on the wall, he put his hunting .22.

"I'll be back for supper."

"You better be," she said. "Just make sure you bring back more flour. I'm usin' the last of it for biscuits for supper."

"Okay," he said.

"And be careful," she said. "Remember—"

"I remember," he said, cutting her off. He didn't have to be reminded of their loved ones who had been killed. It was something he thought about every day.

He left the house, closing the door behind him.

Both Simon and Jesse were in the barn when he started saddling the horse.

"Can we come?" Jesse asked.

"You can't come," Simon said. "You're a girl." He looked at his brother. "I can come, right?"

"You'll both stay here and help your sister," Jason said. "I'll be home for supper."

"What you gonna do, Jason?"

"I'm just gonna get some supplies, Simon."

"And some candy?"

"Maybe."

Jason finished saddling the horse and walked the animal outside. The two little ones followed him out. He slid his Winchester into the scabbard on the saddle.

"You gonna shoot somebody, Jason?" Simon asked, his eyes wide.

"I ain't gonna shoot nobody if I don't have to, Simon," Jason said.

Jason struggled into the saddle, settled himself, grabbed the reins, and then looked down at his eight-year-old brother and six-year-old sister.

"You two do what your sister tells you, understand?" he said. "Don't give her a hard time."

"Bring us some candy!" Jesse yelled.

"I'll do my best."

He jerked the horse's rein to turn it, then kicked it in the sides to get it going.

"I wish I was goin' to town," Jesse said.

"You're a little girl," Simon said. "When you're Jason's age, you can go to town."

She sighed and watched her big brother ride away.

"I wish I was twelve, like him."

TWO

Clint Adams stared across the poker table at trouble.

He had promised himself he would stop playing poker in saloon games. He only wanted to play with true poker players, who knew what they were doing and knew that when they lost, it was because they were outplayed, or luck had gone the wrong way. They never blamed it on somebody cheating.

But he'd been in Santa Rosita for three days while a bone bruise on Eclipse's front hoof healed. Most of the time he was sitting out in front of the hotel, watching the townspeople go by. In the afternoon he went to the saloon for some drinks. In the evening the same small restaurant for supper. In between he checked on Eclipse's progress.

On this day the boredom got to be too much. When he went into the saloon to have a few beers, a poker game was going on in one corner. He watched for as

long as it took him to drink two beers, then walked over.
Before long he was in the game.

Three of the other four players were townspeople. One
owned the mercantile, one was a town alderman, and
the third was a lawyer. The fourth man had just sat in
on the game an hour before Clint. He was passing
through with two friends, who were sitting in another
corner, watching. Clint didn't find out any of this until
he had already sat down and started playing.

It soon became evident that the fourth man, Rutledge,
had the potential to cause trouble. When he lost a hand, it
was always the fault of the cards ("Get me a new deck!")
or a player ("Where'd you learn to deal?"), but it was never
his fault.

The present hand had come down to Clint and Rutledge. They were playing five-card draw. Rutledge had
opened and drawn two cards. From the way he played,
Clint was certain he had three of a kind. From the way
he bet, it was probably something like three fives or
sixes.

Clint had called the bet, drawn one card to the two
pairs he'd been dealt, and had made a full house, jacks
full. Rutledge would have had to draw a fourth six to
beat him. Even if the man made a full house, Clint
doubted he'd be able to beat jacks full.

The stakes had slowly been going up since Clint sat
down: $5 bets had become $20 bets, and $10 had gone
up to $50.

The dealer was Mr. Hackett, the lawyer. He set his
cards down and said, "Mr. Rutledge, it's your bet."

Rutledge looked at his cards again, spreading them,
then folding them in his hands. This was also his tell.

Clint noticed that he folded, spread, folded whenever he had a good hand. But Clint felt sure he had this hand figured correctly. If he didn't, then the man deserved to win it.

"A hundred."

"That's pretty high—" Hackett started, but Rutledge cut him off.

"Ask Mr. Adams if that's too high," he said.

The other three players looked at Clint.

"No, that's fine. If Mr. Rutledge wants to raise the stakes, I have no objection. I'll call the hundred, and raise a hundred."

"This is getting too rich for my blood, gents," said Mason, the mercantile owner. "I'm out of this game after this hand."

"So am I," said Barkley, the alderman.

"Then I guess this is the last hand, gents," Hackett said.

"Then I'll call the hundred and raise another two hundred," Rutledge said.

"That sounds like you've got yourself a good hand, Mr. Rutledge."

"Good enough."

"Well," Clint said, "nobody really wants to go overboard here, so I'll just call that bet."

"No guts?" Rutledge asked. "Afraid to raise?"

"Actually," Clint said, "I'm trying to take it easy on you, Rutledge."

"I don't need you takin' it easy, Adams," Rutledge said. "I got you beat."

"Well," Clint said, "if you promise me you won't be a bad loser . . ."

"I ain't gonna lose at all!" Rutledge said.

"All right . . . how much you got left there?"

Rutledge stared at Clint for a moment, his resolve almost fading, but he firmed his jaw and counted the money in front of him.

"I got two hundred and sixty-five dollars left."

"Then that's the raise," Clint said. "I call your two hundred, and raise two sixty-five."

Folks around the table realized something was going on and got interested. In a few seconds there was a circle around the table. Adding to the interest was the fact that everybody knew who Clint was.

Rutledge stared at Clint for another few minutes, then pushed his money into the pot slowly. He dropped his cards on top of it.

"Sixes full," he said. "Ha! Drew a pair to the three sixes. I call that luck."

"Bad luck," Clint said, laying his cards down. "Jacks full."

"Wha—"

"Adams wins!" Hackett said.

Clint raked the pot in.

"Game's over, gents," Hackett said.

"No," Rutledge said. "No, it ain't. I can get more money."

"No, need, Mr. Rutledge," Hackett said, standing. "This game is done."

Clint was gathering his cash while keeping a wary eye on Rutledge, who had all the earmarks of a terrible loser.

"What the hell kinda deal you call that?" he demanded of Hackett.

"A fair one, Mr. Rutledge," the lawyer said.

"Well," Rutledge said, moving his accusatory look to Clint, "if that was a fair deal, then—"

"Then what, Rutledge?" Clint snapped, cutting him off.

"If I was you, I'd choose my next words real careful."

They all knew Rutledge was about to call Clint a cheater. The people originally circling the table drew back now. The other players cleared out as fast as they could.

"You got something you want to say to me, Rutledge?" Clint demanded.

"Ain't fair, that's all," Rutledge said. "Sixes full shoulda won that pot."

Rutledge—like the two men he rode with—was in his mid-thirties, was wearing dusty trail clothes like they had just come off the range from a cattle drive or something—only there were no cattle drives.

"How's a man get to your age, Rutledge," Clint said, "without knowing that life just ain't always fair? In fact, it's hardly ever fair. And that's just something we all have to live with."

Rutledge stood there, his hands folded into fists.

"You got something else you want to say?" Clint asked.

Rutledge's body shook and then turned on his heel and stalked from the saloon. As the batwing doors swung behind him, his two friends followed him.

THREE

Jason McCall rode into Santa Rosita, stopping briefly to watch some boys his age playing some kind of game with a ball and stick. He wished he could spend time playing with them, but he had an eleven-year-old sister, an eight-year-old brother, and a six-year-old sister who depended on him.

He continued on and reined in only when he was in front of the mercantile store. He dismounted and went inside. He was happy to see that it wasn't Mr. Mason who was behind the counter, but his clerk, Eddie. The clerk was in his late teens, and Jason knew him.

"Hey, Eddie."

"Hello, Jason," Eddie said. "What can I do for you?"

"I need some flour . . ." Jason said, and mindful of how little money he had in his pocket, he mentioned only a few more items.

"Have you got money, Jason?"

"Huh?"

"Mr. Mason says no more credit until you pay what you owe. Actually, he wanted me to tell your father that. Is he around?"

"No," Jason said, "he had to go away to do some work."

"Your mother, then?"

"She's been feelin' poorly," Jason said. "That's why I come to town for the supplies."

"Well . . . you got an outstanding bill, Jason. Can you get some money from your ma?"

"Look, Eddie," Jason said, "Ma's gonna tan my hide if I come home without that flour."

"Jason, I wish I could help—"

Jason reached into his pocket.

"Look," he said, "I got a dollar. I can give you that to put toward our bill. And you can let me have the flour, and some fruit. How about it?"

Jason put the dollar in change on the counter so Eddie could see it.

"I tell you what I'll do," he said, "and Mr. Mason'll probably take some of my hide for doin' it. I'll let you have the flour and a couple of cans of peaches, but that's it. That way at least this dollar will reduce your bill some."

"Okay, Eddie. Thanks."

Eddie swept the change off the counter, then put the flour and peaches into a burlap sack. On the counter was a jar with hard candies in it. He grabbed four of those and dropped them in.

"For you and your sisters," he said. "And your little brother."

"I appreciate it, Eddie."

The clerk held the bag out and said, "You better get out of here before Mr. Mason comes back."

Jason nodded, grabbed the sack, and went outside.

In the saloon Clint gathered his money together and then went to the bar for a beer, which he needed. He was dry, and he never drank while he played poker.

The lawyer, Hackett, came up to him and asked, "Can I buy you that beer?"

"Sure."

Hackett signaled the bartender for two beers.

"I learned a lot from watching you play," Hackett said.

"Well, you paid for the privilege."

"You can say that again," the lawyer said, "but not as much as much as Rutledge paid."

"He's a fool," Clint said. "He insists on playing a game he's not good at, then blames everybody else when he loses."

"If I was you," the lawyer said as the beers were set in front of tem, "I'd watch my step out on the street. He was pretty mad."

"If he comes at me on the street," Clint said, "then he's really a fool."

"He's got two partners with him."

"And they'll be even bigger fools if they follow him," Clint responded.

"How much longer are you staying in town?" Hackett asked.

"I don't know," Clint said. "That depends on how fast my horse is healing."

"Maybe we can get the chance to play again."

"I usually try to stay away from saloon games," Clint said.

"I might be able to set something more private up," Hackett said. "We actually do have some good poker players in town."

"Something private might be okay," Clint said.

"The stakes would be a little higher than today."

"That's okay, too," Clint said. "If I'm still in town, I'd consider it."

"Well, I'll try to set it up and then let you know. Where are you staying?"

"Right across the street," Clint said. "After I finish this beer, I'm going to check on my horse. After that I'll probably be in my room, reading."

"I'll get word to you."

Clint finished his beer, thanked Hackett for it, and headed for the batwings.

Jason came out of the mercantile and tied the burlap bag containing the peaches and flour to his saddle. As he circled the horse, preparing to mount, he saw the three men standing across the street from the saloon. They were all smoking, and watching the front doors. Jason had the feeling something was going to happen, and he didn't want to miss it. He could afford to take a few more minutes before he had to return home and be the big, responsible brother.

He went back onto the boardwalk in front of the mercantile store, found himself a good spot to watch near some barrels, and settled down to wait.

FOUR

"You sure he's comin' out?" Teddy Grant asked Rutledge.

"He'll be out eventually."

"That could take all day," Len Wilson said.

"He's got our money."

"The money we let you talk us into tripling at poker?" Grant asked.

Rutledge gave the man a quick look.

"I woulda tripled it, but Adams cheated."

"How about the fact that he's the Gunsmith?" Wilson asked.

"Does that scare you?" Rutledge asked.

"It sure does."

"You know how good I am with a gun," Rutledge pointed out. "All you know about him is how good he's supposed to be."

Rutledge turned his attention back to the front door of the saloon.

"Today we're gonna find out for sure."

*   *   *

Clint walked to the batwing doors and looked out. Sure enough, across the street was Rutledge, and standing just behind him, to either side, were his two partners.

Hackett came up alongside Clint and looked out.

"Looks like they're waitin' for you."

"Uh-huh."

"You want to go out the back way?"

"No."

"Why not? You could avoid them that way."

"For how long? Besides, if word got out that I ran from a fight, I'd have more fights on my hands than I could handle. I have to face this head on. This is my life."

"I understand. Well, if you have any trouble with the law, I'll represent you."

"Thanks," Clint said.

"Have you met the sheriff?"

"Once," Clint said. "When I realized I was going to be stuck in town, I stopped in to see him."

"What'd you think?"

"He seemed okay."

"That's what he is," Hackett said. "Okay."

Clint didn't think it was time to discuss their opinions about the local lawman.

"You better stay inside."

"I intend to."

Clint nodded, then stepped out the batwing doors.

From where he was, Jason saw the man step out of the saloon. The other three men came to immediate attention. The other man didn't look scared or nothing. Jason was impressed. If he saw three men waiting for him, he would've been really scared.

He moved farther down the street to get a better look, stepped into a doorway to watch.

Clint stopped just outside the batwing doors and looked at the three men.

"You boys waiting for me?" he called.

"You got our money," Rutledge said. "Put it down on the ground and walk away."

"You mean the money I won?"

"I mean the money you cheated me out of."

"You boys let Rutledge play poker with your money? I got some advice for you. Before you do that again, make sure the man you're trusting knows how to play the game."

"I know how to play poker," Rutledge said. "I just don't like gettin' cheated."

"Nobody cheated you, Rutledge," Clint said. "You're just a terrible poker player."

Rutledge looked around to see who was listening to Clint talk to him this way.

"That ain't true!" he snapped.

"Yeah, it is," Clint said. "In fact, you're one of the worst poker players I ever saw. I only sat down because I knew it would be easy to take your money." Clint figured getting the man mad would make him careless. Also, ridiculing him in front of his friends might make them a little less willing to back his play.

"And now that you played lousy and lost," he went on, "you're going to get yourself and your friends killed over it."

"The only one gettin' killed is you."

"Is that because you're better with a gun than you are with cards, Rutledge?" Clint asked. "Boy, you better be."

"That's enough talk," Rutledge said. "Either put our money on the ground and walk away, or go for your gun."

FIVE

Jason watched in rapt attention.

The man who had come out of the saloon was going to face these three men alone. Three against one and he didn't look worried.

But the other men—two of them anyway—looked real worried.

Grant and Wilson were indeed worried.

In fact, both of them were having second thoughts, only they realized it was probably too late. They were going to have to make the most of this bad situation, and hoped they'd have a chance to do it different in the future.

If they had a future.

Clint kept his eyes on Rutledge. He didn't move until the bad poker player did. As it turned out, he was better with his gun than he was with cards . . . but only just.

Jason watched the man draw and fire. It was faster—the fastest thing he'd ever seen. But it was also accurate. He shot each of the three men once, and they all fell to the ground, dead.

He had to get closer.

The sheriff may have just been okay in Hackett's opinion, but he was on the scene within moments of the shots.

"Adams," he said. "I shoulda knowed it."

"Sheriff Dyson," Clint said.

The sheriff was in his forties, a weary-looking man who had spent his life going from town to town, never wearing the badge for very long before moving on—for one reason or another.

"What was this about?" Dyson asked.

Clint pointed to Rutledge.

"That one was a bad loser at poker," he said. "The other two were his partners. They were waiting for me when I came out."

"I can guess the rest," Dyson said. He looked past Clint at the saloon, where people were standing in the windows, watching. There was one man standing at the batwing doors.

"I suppose Hackett saw the whole thing?"

"Yes."

"Okay," Dyson said. "I'll just need a statement from you, and a witness statement from Hackett."

"I was a witness."

They both turned to see who had spoken. Clint saw a skinny red-haired boy of about twelve or thirteen.

"Jason, what are you doin' in town?" Sheriff Dyson asked.

"Pickin' up some supplies," the boy said. "Those men were waitin' for him. He didn't have no choice."

"Thank you, Jason," Clint said. "My name's Clint Adams."

He put his hand out for the boy to shake. After a moment the boy took it, then shook it once. He was staring at Clint with his mouth open.

"The Gunsmith?" he finally asked.

"That's right."

"We don't need you as a witness, Jason," Dyson said. "You better go on home. Your parents will be worried about you."

"But—"

"Go."

The boy made a face, then turned and walked to his horse. He was short, so he had to struggle to get mounted. When he finally did, he reluctantly rode out of town.

"Nice kid," Clint said.

"Lives outside of town with his parents, and three other kids. I'm gonna go in the saloon, talk to Hackett, and get me some men to move these bodies."

"I'm going to go and check on my horse," Clint said, "then I'll be in my room."

"Come by later today and make a statement," Dyson said. "Won't take long."

"I'll stop by before supper."

"Fine."

Dyson walked toward the hotel. He stopped at the batwings to exchange a few words with Hackett, who nodded and then waved at Clint.

Clint waved back, looked down at the three bodies, then walked to the livery.

SIX

"It was a bad one," the liveryman, Rufus, said. "Still ain't healed."

Clint knew the stone bruise on Eclipse's hoof was bad from the way the big Darley Arabian had been limping. Eclipse was an iron horse, didn't usually react to any injury unless it was really bad.

"He's gonna need a few more days," Rufus said.

"How's he eating?" Clint asked.

"Like a horse." Rufus grinned, but when Clint didn't laugh, he went on. "He's feedin' real good. The injury ain't hurt his appetite. He ain't gonna lose no weight."

"That's good."

They were standing near the horse's stall so Clint reached out and patted Eclipse's rump.

"Get better, big boy," he said. He looked at Rufus. "I'll check back in tomorrow."

"Hey, I heard some shootin'," Rufus said. "That have anythin' to do with you?"

"Yeah," Clint said, "it may have had something to do with me."

Jason rode home as quickly as he could, dismounted, and ran into the house. Jesse, Simon, and Jenny were all there. The two little ones were watching Jenny take something out of the stove.

"Jace," Jesse yelled, "Jenny made a chokecherry pie."

"We helped pick the chokecherries," Simon said.

"That's great," Jesse said. He looked at Jenny. "We gotta talk." Then he looked at Jesse and Simon. "You guys go outside and play."

"We wanna eat pie," Simon said.

"It has to cool down," Jenny told them. "I'll call you when it's ready."

"Okay!" they yelled, and ran outside.

Jenny looked at Jason.

"What's wrong?"

"Ain't nothin' wrong," Jason said.

"Did you get the flour?"

"Yeah, I got the flour, and some peaches, and I got some candy for the kids."

"How'd you do that with a dollar?"

"I'll tell you later," he said. "I got to tell you somethin' else. What I saw."

"What did you see?"

"Come and sit down," he said, pulling her to the table. "Sit down and I'll tell ya."

They sat at the table, across from each other, and Jason took Jenny's hands in his.

"I found him," she said. "I found the man who can find Papa for us."

"What? Where? What did you see?"

"I saw him," Jason said, "the Gunsmith. I saw him shoot three men in the street, just like that. All by himself."

"What? Did you get hurt?"

"No, no," he said, "I wasn't nowhere near. I just watched."

"And it was the Gunsmith?" she asked. "The real Gunsmith?"

"It was him," Jason said. "I been waitin' for our chance, Jenny, and this is it."

"Is he gonna do it?" she asked.

"I didn't ask him," Jason said. "I wanted to come and tell you first."

"So when are you gonna ask him?"

"Tomorrow."

"But . . . he won't do it for nothin', will he?" she asked.

"That's why I wanted to talk to you," he said.

He got up from the table, went to the stone fireplace, and pulled off a loose stone. He reached in, found his treasure, and drew it out. He took it back to the table with him.

It was a small bag, made of some sort of animal hide. It had been his father's. He loosened the leather thong holding it closed, upended it, and let the money drop out, coins and paper.

"Jason!" she exclaimed. "Where did you get all that money?"

"I been savin' it," he said.

"You mean . . . you had this all along? You know how much food we coulda bought with this?"

"It's not for food," Jason said. "It's to find Papa."

She touched the money with her index finger, moving it around on the table.

"How much is there?"

"Nineteen dollars and fifty-eight cents," he said.

"I ain't never seen this much money before."

"I was hopin' ta get it to twenty dollars," Jason said. "I think the Gunsmith would do it for twenty dollars. Don't you?"

"Anybody would do anythin' for twenty dollars," she said, "but will he do it for nineteen dollars and fifty-eight cents?"

"I don't know," Jason said. "I'll ask him tomorrow."

SEVEN

The next morning Clint was having breakfast when the boy walked into the café. He spotted Clint and came rushing over.

"Mr. Adams?"

"Jason, right?"

"Yeah."

"What can I do for you, Jason?"

"I gotta talk to you . . . sir."

"Well, sit down," Clint said. "Have some breakfast."

Jason looked at Clint's steak and eggs, and his mouth began to water.

"I can't, sir."

"Why not?"

"It wouldn't be right," Jason said. "My brother and my sisters, they ain't ate this good in a long time."

"Where are they?"

"Outside, in the buckboard. They're gonna stay there while I talk to you."

"Bring 'em in, son," Clint said. "I'll buy all of you breakfast."

"You mean it?"

"I do."

The boy ran outside and came running back in with his sisters and brother. The other diners in the place stared at them as they sat with Clint Adams.

"Introduce me," Clint said.

"That's Jenny, Simon, and Jesse."

"Hello."

They all nodded, stared at the food on his plate.

Clint waved the waitress over. She was a pretty woman in her thirties who had waited on him each time he came in. Her name was Amy.

"These aren't your kids," she said.

"No."

"Wait," she said, "you're the McCall kids."

They all looked at her guiltily.

"You know them?" Clint asked.

"I know the family," she said. "But nobody has seen their mother or father for some time."

"Bring them all the same thing I have," Clint said.

"Comin' up."

He looked around, saw the stares they were drawing.

"What's the matter with everyone?"

"The McCall family . . . they're not exactly well liked in town."

"Well, these are just kids," he said, "and I'm feeding them."

"Comin' up," she said again.

Clint looked around at the four young faces staring at him.

"Are you really the Gunsmith?" Jenny asked.

"Yes, I am."

"Wow!" Simon said.

"Yeah," Jesse said, "wow." Clint was sure from the way she was looking around the table, she had no idea who he was.

"What was it you wanted to talk to me about, Jason?" Clint asked.

"It's about our father," Jason said. "His name is Jimmy."

"Jimmy McCall?" Clint asked.

All four of them nodded.

"I'm afraid I never heard of him."

"That's okay," Jason said, "he ain't famous, or nothin'."

"He's just our dad," Jenny said.

"Well, where is he?" Clint asked.

"That's what we want you to find out," Jason said. He took the bag out of his pocket and put it on the table.

"What's this?" Clint picked it up, heard the change jingle.

"That's nineteen dollars and fifty-eight cents," Jason said.

"That's a lot!" Simon said.

"It's a fortune," Jenny said.

"I'm hungry," Jesse said.

On cue the waitress came over with four plates she carried up and down her arms. She set one plate in front of each child.

"I'll go get a basket of warm biscuits," she said.

"Wow!" Simon said.

"Okay," Clint said, "go ahead and eat. We can keep talking while we eat."

"Yessir!" Jason said.

All four kids picked up their forks and dug in.

"Where is your mother?" Clint asked.

"Ma died," Jason said.

"When?"

"Months ago."

"And what did your father do?" he asked.

"Well," Jason said, his mouth full of eggs and steak, "at first he cried a lot, but then he told us he had to go away."

"Where?"

"He wouldn't tell us," Jenny said, "but he said when he came back, we'd have all the money we need."

"And how long ago was this?" Clint asked.

She looked at her old brother.

"A few months."

"Wait a minute," Clint said. "Have you kids been living by yourselves all this time?"

They didn't answer, but all four of them looked guilty.

"You have, haven't you?" Clint said. "And you haven't let anybody know."

"No sir," Jason said.

"Why not?"

"They'd split us up if they knew," Jenny said.

"So how have you been living?" Clint asked.

"I do odd jobs," Jason said, "and I hunt."

"I been cookin' and cleanin'," Jenny said.

"And me and Jesse do chores," Simon said.

Jesse made a face and said, "I hate doin' chores."

"Lots of people do, Jesse," Clint said.

Amy came back with a tray bearing a basket of

biscuits and four glasses of milk. She set them out on the table.

"I'll get you some more coffee, Mr. Adams."

"Thanks, Amy," he said, "and just call me Clint."

"All right, Clint."

"Can we call you Clint?" Simon asked.

"Simon!" Jenny said. "Have some respect. You call him Mr. Adams."

Clint was going to contradict her, then decided against it.

They all continued to eat.

"So, Jason, your father didn't say where he was going."

"No sir."

"Did he say who he was going with?"

"He did mention a name."

"What name?"

"Donovan."

"Are you sure?" Clint asked.

Jason looked at Jenny.

"I heard it, too," she said.

"Donovan," Clint said.

"Do you know him?" Jason asked.

"If it's the same man," Clint said, "I'm afraid I do."

EIGHT

The kids finished eating. Clint made sure they had enough, asked if they wanted more. The two young ones seemed poised to ask for more, but a look from their eleven-year-old sister held them in check.

"We've all had enough, Mr. Adams," Jason said, "and we thank you. But we'd like to know if you're gonna find our dad for us."

"Well," Clint said, "first I want you to take this back." Clint pushed the bag containing the nineteen dollars and fifty-eight cents back across the table to Jason.

Jenny asked, "Does this mean you ain't gonna look for—"

"Jenny," Clint said, "I just want you to have your money back. Use it to buy some food and supplies. As for your father, I want to take a ride out to your house with you. We'll finish talking about it out there. How's that sound?"

"Well," she said, "I ain't cleaned the place up—"

"Don't worry about it," Clint said. "Come on. Meet me outside after I pay the bill."

The four kids stood up and walked out of the restaurant. The other diners followed their progress with their eyes.

"What's wrong with you people?" Clint asked as he stood. "They're just a bunch of kids."

"McCall kids," a man said.

Clint ignored him. Amy came over and he handed her money for the breakfast.

"Don't think too badly of these people, Clint," she said. "The McCalls have never been very neighborly to them."

"That's no reason to mistreat their kids," Clint said.

"I feel bad for them," she said, "especially the little ones. Let me know what happens, okay?"

"I will, Amy."

He stepped outside, found all the kids already loaded onto the buckboard. Jason and the small ones were in the back, while Jenny was on the seat.

"You can sit here, Clint," she said, tapping the space next to her.

"Thanks," he said. He climbed up next to her. "You mind if I drive?"

She handed him the reins.

"How far do you live?" he asked. "Will I be able to walk back?"

"It's pretty far," Simon said.

"But you could walk it," Jason said.

"I got short legs," Simon added.

"Yes, you do, little guy," Clint said. "Okay, give me directions."

* * *

Clint drove the buckboard to the McCall house, a run-down shack just outside of town. Actually, the horse pretty much knew the way, so he just gave the animal his head.

"This is our house!" Simon shouted as he jumped down from the buckboard.

"I can see that," Clint said. He got down, helped Jenny down, and then lifted Jesse down from the back. Jason dropped to the ground.

"Come on," Jason said. "I'll show you the inside."

Clint looked around at the coral and barn that were in need of repair, then followed the kids into the house, hoping it wouldn't fall down around them.

The inside was as bad as the outside. The furniture that was there was in pieces, torn curtains hung on the windows, some of which were broken.

"This is where you live?"

"It looked a lot better when Ma and Pa were here," Jenny told him.

Clint looked at Jason.

"Why not send the little ones out to play, Jason," he suggested.

"Jesse, Simon, here," Jason said. He gave them each a piece of the hard candy he had brought home for them the day before. "Go out and play."

"Okay," Simon said. "Come on, Jesse!"

The two little ones ran out.

"Let's sit," Clint said to Jenny and Jason.

They all sat at the rickety kitchen table.

"Jason, what did your dad take with him when he left?" Clint asked.

"His gun, his rifle, his saddlebags, and the only good saddle horse that we had."

"And what did he tell you?"

"That I was in charge of my brother and my sisters," Jason said.

"He said Jason had to be the daddy, and I had to be the mommy, until he came back," Jenny said.

"And that's what we done," Jason said.

"But Papa's been gone too long," Jenny said with tears in her eyes. "We miss him. Simon and Jesse, they miss him."

"I can't go look for them, Mr. Adams," Jason said. "I can look after my brother, and my sisters, but I know I'm too small, too young to go and find him. So I been saving money until I could find somebody to go and find him for us."

"And that's me?"

"I saw what you done yesterday, in front of the saloon," Jason said. "You ain't afraid of nothin'. You can do anythin'."

"You can do it, Mr. Adams," Jenny said. "You got to!"

"We need our pa," Jason said.

"Yes, you do," Clint said. "You do need your father."

"Then you'll do it?" Jenny asked.

"If you'll call me Clint," he said to her, "I'll do it."

"Oh, Clint." She got up, ran around the table, and threw her arms around his neck.

What had he got himself into this time?

NINE

Clint walked back to town and stopped in at Sheriff Dyson's office.

"You here to make your statement?" Dyson asked. "I expected you last night."

"Sorry," Clint said. "I can do it now, but I really came here to talk to you about something else."

"About what?"

"Jason McCall's father," he said.

"Jimmy? What about him?"

"What can you tell me about him?"

"Jimmy's ornery," Dyson said. "He has no friends. Him and his wife lived out there with their kids, only came to town for supplies. And then his wife died."

"Naturally?"

"Yeah," Dyson said. "She just got sick and . . . died."

"Then what happened?"

"Jimmy didn't take it well," Dyson said. "He started

to drink, neglected the house, the barn, the kids . . . Why are you askin'?"

"The kids . . . they asked me to talk to him," Clint said.

"I don't know what good that'll do," Dyson said. "I don't even think he'll talk to you. He'll probably take a shot at you if you go out there."

Clint didn't tell the sheriff he'd already been out there. He promised the kids he wouldn't tell anybody that Jimmy had gone. Those four kids really did belong together, so he promised he wouldn't let them get split up, if he could help it.

"Is Jimmy a lawbreaker, Sheriff?"

"Naw, not really."

"What do you mean by 'not really'?"

"Well . . . if Jimmy saw a way to make an easy buck, he might take it," Dyson said. "He does love those kids, so . . ."

"So he'd do something against the law to take care of them?"

"Well . . . I guess that's what any father would do," Dyson said.

"Yeah, okay," Clint said. "Give me some paper. I'll write out that statement you need and sign it."

"Okay," Dyson said. He got the paper and pencil from his desk and pushed it over to Clint.

After Clint had written out his statement and signed it, he left the sheriff's office.

"Good luck with Jimmy," Dyson said.

"Yeah, thanks."

"And make sure you let me know when you leave town, will ya?"

"I will."

But Clint couldn't leave, not until Eclipse was ready to travel. When he did leave, he promised the kids he'd look for their father.

But if Jimmy McCall had gotten involved with Donovan, then he definitely was in a position to break the law.

Andy Donovan was an outlaw, the leader of an outlaw band. He had a reputation as a thief, a gunman, a killer. And anybody who rode with him was also a thief, and probably a killer.

But Jimmy McCall had four kids and, according to the sheriff, wasn't a thief or a murderer, just a dad trying to take care of his kids.

But if he was riding with Donovan, Clint wasn't sure he could bring him back alive.

TEN

Clint went to see Amy as she was getting off work. She was surprised to see him when she came outside.

"How did you know when I finished work?" she asked.

"I saw you going home one night," he said. "Can I walk you?"

"Well . . . sure."

"I want to talk to you about those kids," I said, "and their parents."

"Are they okay?" she asked while they walked.

"Yes, they're fine. Did you know their mother?" he asked.

"Kate," she said, "yes, I knew her. I think I might've been her only friend. I was so sorry when she died. I tried to help them, but Jimmy chased me off. He wouldn't let me come out there."

Clint had the feeling Jimmy was keeping everybody

away from the house because he knew he was going to leave, and he didn't want anyone to go out there and see that the kids were alone.

He had to choose his words carefully with Amy.

"Tell me about Jimmy," he said.

"Jimmy loved Kate, and he loves those kids," she said. "He's just been a wreck since she died. Do the kids think you can do something about him?"

"I don't know," he said. "I think they just want me to talk to him. Jason seems to think he can trust me."

"I'd trust you," she said.

"You don't even know me."

"I have found that Jason is a good judge of character," she said.

"How's Jimmy's character, Amy?"

"What do you mean?"

"Would he break the law to help his kids?"

"In a minute. If only he'd stop drinking," she said. "He hasn't been to town in weeks."

"You haven't tried to go back out there?"

"Jimmy made himself pretty clear the last time," she said. "No, I haven't tried to go back."

"And nobody else has?"

"Jimmy doesn't have any friends, Clint," she said. "He's sort of made sure of that."

"I see."

"Well, here I am," she said. "Do you want to come in and have a look?"

They were standing in front of the building that housed the hardware store. He assumed she was talking about something upstairs.

"Um, aren't you afraid . . ." he started, looking around.

"Don't worry about my reputation," she said. "I don't. Come on. I want to show you my bedroom."

"Your bedroom?"

She linked her arm in his and said, "I've been wanting to get you into my bedroom since that first day you came in."

"Amy—"

"Don't tell me you're shy."

"No, I'm not shy."

"Well, I'm not either," she said. "And I get the feeling you're not gonna be in town much longer. This may be my last chance."

She slid her hand down to his and clasped it.

"Are you comin' up?"

He smiled at her and said, "I'm coming up."

Clint had been to bed with waitresses before, and they all had one thing in common. They smelled like the food they served. He never considered that a bad thing. He'd also been to bed with them right after they left work, and there were other smells he didn't mind. In fact, he liked when he could smell a woman's sweat. And at the end of the day a woman smelled like a woman. Amy had all of that, and more.

She led him into her bedroom, released his hand, turned, and removed her dress in record time. She stood naked in front of him, gave him time to take a good, long look.

She was medium height, maybe five-four, had full

breasts with heavy undersides and large nipples. They were perfect as far as he was concerned.

He moved close to her, took her in his arms, and kissed her. She pressed her breasts tightly against his chest. He let his hands glide over her back until he was cupping her buttocks. She moaned into his mouth as the kiss went on and on . . .

Finally, she backed away, but only far enough to allow her to get her hands on his belt. He helped her by removing his gun belt, setting it aside within easy reach. After that she had no problem removing the rest of his clothes.

Naked, he stepped back to take another look at her. Her ass, legs, and thighs were powerfully built from all those years spent on her feet, waiting tables. In her thirties her breasts were sagging only slightly, and that was more from their weight than from age.

They sank onto the bed together in a hot embrace, kissing, touching, tasting. Her skin was smooth and hot, the muscles beneath it rippling. He kissed her neck, her shoulders, the slopes of her breasts, then concentrated on her nipples with his tongue and teeth. She sighed, groaned, held his head to her breasts until he yanked it away to go lower.

His mouth traced a wet trail over her ribs and belly, and as he dipped even lower, she opened her legs wide to allow him access. He kissed her thighs, nuzzled his nose into her pubic region, inhaling the variety of scents there. In the morning there might have been a single smell, just her natural scent, but at the end of the workday she was savory sweet and slightly sour both to his nose, and his tongue.

He tasted her, licking her lovingly until she was soaking, then sliding his tongue inside her, making her jump.

"Oooh," she said, "I can feel all the tension of the day melting away."

He spread her labia with his thumbs and said, "Now let's work on the tensions of the week."

ELEVEN

Jimmy McCall drained his whiskey glass, then lifted the bottle and refilled it.

"You don't wanna drink too much of that stuff, Jimmy boy," Andy Donovan warned him. "It'll knock you on your ass."

Ted Drake laughed uproariously until Donovan stopped him with a stare.

"Maybe I don't care," McCall said.

"Jimmy, I can't have you bein' too hungover tomorrow," Donovan said. "We got a job to do."

McCall looked over at the other four men who were standing at the bar, drinking and laughing.

"What about them?" he asked.

"Them? They're always hungover. They work better that way. You, Jimmy, I need you to be thinkin' straight. They don't have to think to do what they do. They wouldn't be very good at it anyway."

McCall shrugged and started to lift the glass. Donovan put his big hand on the other man's forearm, stopping him.

"Look, I know you're sorry you left your kids, and you feel guilty about it. I know you wanna see them again. You miss 'em. They're probably cute little tykes. But look at it this way. When you do go back home, you'll be taking a lot of money with you."

"And when will I be seein' some of that money, Andy?" McCall asked. "Some of this money you told me I'd be makin' if I joined you?"

Donovan looked at Drake.

"Go to the bar and tell those idiots to stop drinkin'," he said.

"But you just said—"

"I know what I said," Donovan snapped. "Just go tell them to stop drinkin' and start fuckin'. They won't mind that so much."

"Gotcha, boss."

Drake got up and walked over to the bar to join the other men.

"Jimmy," Donovan said, "we'll be splittin' our profits soon. But why don't you face it? If I had given you any before now, you probably would've drunk it all away."

McCall gave that a moment's thought, figured Donovan was probably right. The big man removed his hand and McCall downed the whiskey.

"Why don't you go to the cathouse and fuck for a while?" Donovan asked.

McCall filled his glass gloomily.

"Oh wait," Donovan said, "you're still mournin' your wife, right?"

McCall drank. Reminding him of his dead wife was not the way to stop him from drinking.

"Jimmy, Jimmy . . ."

"Andy, relax," McCall said. "I'm the one member of this gang that you can count on and you know it."

"I do know it," Donovan said. "That's why I want you sober."

"Why don't you go and do some fuckin'?" McCall asked. "I'll be goin' to my room soon."

"Yeah, you're right," Donovan said. "I could use some time in the sack with a woman. Maybe two."

He looked over at the bar. The men had obviously taken his suggestion, because they were all gone—including Ted Drake.

"Okay, Jimmy," he said, standing, "I'll take you at your word. You'll be sober and ready come mornin'."

"You have my word, Andy."

Donovan slapped McCall on the back and left the saloon. McCall poured himself another drink.

TWELVE

Clint slid his hard cock up into Amy's wet pussy, virtually gliding home. She wrapped those powerful thighs around his waist and he proceeded to fuck her hard. They'd been gentle with each other long enough. Now was the time to just take what they wanted from each other.

She matched his rhythm, lifting her hips each time he drove into her, so that the room filled not only with the smells of sex, but the sound of wet flesh slapping wet flesh.

"Oh, yes, come on," she grunted, pulling on him, scratching his back, doing what she could to urge him on and on . . .

Her breath began coming in hard gulps, and then suddenly he felt her body tense, and then spasm. She cried out and then he followed, bellowing out loud as he erupted inside her. He came in hard spurts, and when he thought he was done, she continued to milk him with her insides, until it was an exquisite combination of pleasure and pain . . .

Clint left Amy's room while she was still dozing in bed. He thought he might return later, rather than sleep in his hotel room. She was quite a girl.

He stopped in the nearest saloon, a small one called the Silver Spur, and had a leisurely beer at the bar. After a few moments a man entered and joined him at the bar. It was the lawyer, Hackett.

"There you are," he said. "I've been looking for you."

"Buy you a beer?" Clint asked.

"Why not?"

Clint signaled the bartender for two more.

"What's on your mind?"

"That poker game I promised you?" Hackett said. "I'm having some trouble coming up with players."

"That's okay," Clint said. "I may not be around that much longer."

"Oh?" Hackett said. "Is the sheriff running you out of town?"

"No, nothing like that," Clint said. "Just time to be on my way."

"I see," Hackett said. He finished the beer, set the empty mug down. "Well, I'm sorry we couldn't square off again at the table. Maybe another time."

"Maybe," Clint said. "Oh, and by the way, thanks for the help with the sheriff."

"No trouble," Hackett said. "I just told him what I saw."

Hackett waved and left the Spur.

* * *

Jenny got out of her bed, saw her brother Jason standing by the front door. The door was open and he was staring out.

"Jason, what's wrong?" she asked.

"Nothin'."

She came up alongside him.

"Somethin's on your mind."

"I just wish I could go lookin' for Pa myself," he said.

"We need you here, Jace," she said, taking hold of his arm.

He looked at her and said, "I know. It's just . . . he's out there somewhere, probably in trouble, tryin' to get some money for us. I just wanna help him."

"You are," she said. "You're helpin' him by takin' care of us."

He looked back out the door.

"Clint will find him," she said. "I know he will."

"I wish he could leave right away."

"He'll go as soon as his horse can," she said. "I trust him, Jace."

He looked at his sister again.

"You better get some sleep."

"You, too."

"I will," he said. "I promise."

The cabin had two bedrooms. Jenny shared one with her sister, Jesse. Jason shared the other one with Simon.

Jason stood in the doorway a few minutes longer, then closed it and went back to his room. He tried to get into the bed he shared with his brother without waking Simon, but the boy stirred.

"What's goin' on?" he asked.

"Nothin'," Jason said, "go back to sleep." He settled on his back.

"Jace?"

"Yeah?"

"You ain't gonna leave us, are ya?"

Jason turned his head to look at his little brother.

"What makes you think I'd leave you, Simon?"

"Ma left," the boy said, "and Pa left."

"Ma died, Simon," Jason said, "and Pa's comin' back. And I ain't leavin'."

"Promise?"

"Yeah, I promise. Go to sleep."

"Yes, Jace."

Simon closed his eyes.

Jason stared at the ceiling for about ten minutes, and then his eyes closed.

THIRTEEN

Clint went back to Amy's later that evening and knocked on the door. She opened the door and smiled at him.

"I was hoping you'd come back," she said. "Are you hungry?"

"I could eat."

"Come in," she said. "I have something on the stove."

He walked in and took a deep breath.

"It smells great."

"Stew," she said. "I made it myself. Sit."

He sat at the table and she returned with two bowls of fragrant, dark stew.

"Coffee?"

"Please."

She set it in front of him.

"I made it the way you like it," she said. "Dark and strong."

"Wow," he said after one taste, "this stew is great."

"Secret ingredient," she said.

"What is it?"

"If I told you," she said, "it wouldn't be a secret, would it?"

"I guess not."

"So just shut up and eat it."

He did both.

They sat together later on her sofa with coffee.

"I feel bad for those kids," she said.

"So do I."

She looked at him.

"Do you think you'll be able to find him?"

"Find who?"

"I'm not stupid, Clint," she said. "I know Jimmy left. They want you to find him and bring him back, right?"

"Well . . ."

"I'm not going to tell anyone," she said. "I know those kids don't want to be split up."

"I think I can find him."

"How?"

"Jason had one piece of helpful information."

"And what was that?"

"He said his dad talked about a man named Donovan."

"And that was helpful?"

"If he was talking about Andy Donovan, then yeah," Clint said.

"Who's Andy Donovan?"

"An outlaw," Clint said, "and if Jimmy McCall joined his band of cutthroats, then he's in trouble."

"Jimmy's no outlaw," she said. "I mean, he's not perfect, but he's no cutthroat."

"Maybe not," Clint said, "but if he rides with them, it could be just as bad. And there's another thing I know about Donovan."

"What's that?"

"He doesn't like to share," Clint said. "He'd kill his own men for a bigger share of the loot."

"What loot?"

"Whatever loot they're after," Clint said. "Banks, stagecoaches, trains, Donovan doesn't care."

"Jimmy is smart, Clint," she said, "but he doesn't always make the right decision."

"Then I guess he's running true to form," he said. "Riding with Andy Donovan is never a good choice."

"But . . . how would he know such a man?"

"I don't know," Clint said. "Maybe they're old friends."

"If they were, would Donovan still kill him?"

"Donovan would kill his own mother for a bigger cut," Clint said.

"Jesus," she said, "then I guess you better find him and bring him back to those kids."

"That's what I intend to do."

"When?"

"I'll check on my horse tomorrow, see if he's ready to go," Clint said.

"And if he isn't?"

"I might just have to rent a horse," he said, "although I prefer a mount I can count on. Especially if I have to go up against Andy Donovan and his boys."

"And you're gonna do this for nineteen dollars and fifty-eight cents?"

"No," Clint said, "I'm going to do it for those kids. I told them to keep the money, spend it on supplies."

"So you'll use your own money to rent a horse?"

"I won't have much choice," he said.

"I wish I had some money to give you."

"I have all the money I need. Plus it's not your responsibility."

"It's not yours either," she said, "but you're gonna do it anyway."

"Somebody's got to help those kids," Clint said. "They can't keep living out there alone. If I don't bring their father back, something's going to have to be done."

"They'll be split up."

"They'll probably be better off."

She snuggled up closer to him, put her head on his shoulder.

"You tell me when you're leavin'," she said. "I'll look out for them until you get back."

"Okay," he said, putting his arms around her, "that'll work. We'll deal with the rest when I get back, with or without their father."

FOURTEEN

The next morning Clint awoke on the sofa with Amy still lying on him. He slid out from beneath her without waking her, and left. When he got to the livery, Rufus was already there, working.

"Rufus, I need my horse," he said.

The older man looked at him, then said, "Well, let's take a look."

They went to Eclipse's stall and lifted his leg to look at the hoof.

"It's not too bad," Rufus said.

"I need to ride, Rufus," Clint said. "I need my horse. What can you do to protect that spot?"

"Well," Rufus said, "I can put another shoe on, a thicker one, with a, sort of, shield. So's he don't bruise that same spot."

"Okay," Clint said, "okay, do that. When can you have it done?"

"This afternoon," Rufus said. "You can have him at noon."

"Okay," Clint said. "Noon it is. Thanks, Rufus."

Clint went to the mercantile to pick up a few supplies, just enough so that he could carry them with him without a packhorse. After that he went to the telegraph office and sent off a couple of telegrams. His two most trustworthy sources for information were his friend Rick Hartman in Labyrinth, Texas, and the private detective Talbot Roper in Denver. He asked them both if they had any information about the whereabouts of Andy Donovan and his gang. He hoped to have almost immediate responses. Getting one from Hartman probably wouldn't be a problem, since the man rarely left Labyrinth. Tal Roper, however, might be away from Denver on a case. It remained to be seen.

At noon Clint returned to the livery to collect Eclipse. Rufus had him saddled and ready to go.

"He's movin' pretty well," he said, "but I wouldn't push him."

"I'll try not to."

He decided to walk the Darley Arabian out to the McCall house to talk to the kids before he left. He found all four of them outside, doing chores.

"Wow!" Simon said when he spotted them coming. "Is that your horse?"

"He sure is."

"What's his name?"

"Eclipse."

"He's beautiful," Jesse said with shining eyes.

The two small ones approached Eclipse, who lowered his head so they could pet him.

"Jesse, Simon, be careful," Jenny called.

"It's all right," Clint said. "He won't hurt children."

Jason came walking over.

"Are you leavin'?"

"Gettin' ready to." He pointed to the burlap bag he had tied to his saddle. "I've got some supplies. I'm just waiting for a couple of telegrams that may help me find your dad."

"Really?" Jenny asked. "You might find him fast?"

"I don't know about fast," he told her, "but I'll find him. You and Jason just have to make sure you take care of your brother and sister."

"We will," Jenny said.

"Amy, from the café, will be coming out to check on you from time to time."

"You told her—" Jason started to accuse him.

"I didn't have to tell her anything," Clint said. "She knew your father was gone. And she won't tell anybody. She's just going to come out and see that you're doing okay."

"We don't need no checkin' up on," Jason said sullenly.

"Well, you're going to get it," Clint said, "and you better be polite to her. She might even bring you some food."

"Yummy," Simon said.

"Okay," Jason said to his siblings, "everybody back to work."

They all went back to what they were doing before Clint arrived.

Jason moved up closer so that his brother and sisters wouldn't hear him.

"Clint," he said, keeping his voice low, "if you find our pa and he's dead, you'll tell me, right?"

"Of course I'll tell you," Clint said. "I'll come back here and tell you, Jason. I won't send you a telegram."

"That's good," Jason said, "but you gotta tell me, and then I'll tell them."

"Let's deal with that if it happens, Jason," Clint said. "No sense thinking the worst."

"A-All right."

"You're a good man, Jason," Clint said. "Watch out for your family."

"Yes, sir," Jason said, "I will."

FIFTEEN

When Clint got to the telegraph office, the clerk had two responses for him. He accepted them, took them outside to read.

Rick Hartman's telegram said the last he heard Donovan and his crew were in Texas. He couldn't be more specific, but he said it was not South Texas.

On the other hand, Talbot Roper not only said Texas, but North Texas. He also warned Clint that the man probably had a crew of seven or more.

Clint folded both telegrams and stuffed them into his shirt pocket. At that moment the sheriff came walking along.

"Bad news?" he asked.

"Good news for you," Clint said. "I'm about to mount up and ride out."

"For good?"

"For a while," Clint said. "I'll be back, but I'm not sure when."

"Well," the sheriff said, "watch your back trail."

"I always do."

The sheriff walked away. Clint stepped down from the boardwalk, mounted Eclipse, and rode out of town.

Jimmy McCall came out of the Trail Dust Café and stretched. He missed his kids. He didn't have enough money yet to go back to them. In fact, he didn't have any money at all yet.

Andy Donovan was hanging on tight to all the loots he and his crew—including Jimmy—had stolen over the past few months. Nothing Jimmy said to him could get him to let some of it go. He knew Donovan's reputation. But he also knew some men who had worked for Donovan made money and left him. Alive.

Donovan had the rest of his crew convinced that all they had to do was follow him, obey him, and they'd all be rich.

Eventually.

Jimmy didn't want to be rich. He just wanted to have enough money to go back to Santa Rosita and take proper care of his kids. He'd left Jason in charge, and the poor kid was having to grow up too fast.

Jimmy's belly was full after a flapjack breakfast. He walked down the street and took up his position across the street from the bank. It was anybody's guess if Donovan and his crew were going to be sober enough to pull this off.

Donovan woke up next to a full-bodied brunette whom he had ridden hard all night. Now, as she lay on her back next to him, snoring, he realized she looked a lot like a horse.

He swung his feet to the floor and stood up, naked. He rubbed his hands over his face, then looked back at the woman on the bed again. He wondered what he had seen in her last night. Possibly the big, floppy tits with dark brown nipples? Or maybe the wild tangle of black hair between her legs? She opened her mouth then, and he knew it wasn't the big oversized teeth that had attracted him.

He turned away and looked down at his own body. His belly wasn't as flat as it used to be, and the hair on his chest was starting to turn gray. His penis, now flaccid, still performed fine when it was hard, if the horsey whore's screams were any indication.

He was still staring down at himself when suddenly a hand appeared and cupped his genitals.

"Where ya goin'?" she asked.

"Time to get up."

She moved her hand up and gripped his penis. It immediately began to swell.

"Are you sure?" she asked, stroking him.

"Well . . ."

"Turn around," she said. "I want to do somethin' while you're tryin' to decide."

He turned and she took his cock deep into her horsey mouth. As he rose up onto his toes, he remembered why he had picked her . . .

The rest of the crew was already on the street with their horses when Donovan came out of the whorehouse.

"Have your ashes hauled for breakfast, boss?" one of them asked.

"Shut up," Donovan said. "Where's my horse?"

"Back here." One of the men rode up to him, leading his sorrel. He mounted up.

"Everybody know what they're supposed to do?"

"We know," Henry Carter said, and the others nodded.

"Everybody sober enough?"

"Almost," Carter answered. "Benny's still pretty drunk."

"Benny, you'll stay with the horses. We don't need you shootin' one of us by accident."

Listing to one side on his horse, Benny said, "Sure, boss."

"What about Jimmy?" Carter asked.

"If I know Jimmy, he's in position," Donovan said.

"Still don't know why we need him," Carter said, miffed. He was Donovan's second in command, his *segundo*, but he didn't feel like it since Jimmy joined up.

"We need him," Donovan said, "because he's smarter than the rest of you jokers put together."

The men exchanged glances, but no one really seemed to have taken offense, except perhaps for Carter.

"All right, check your guns."

There was a succession of clicks and spins as the outlaws drew their revolvers and made sure they were fully loaded.

"Okay," Donovan said, "we've done this plenty of times before, so there shouldn't be any problems. As usual, if any of you make a mess of this, I'll shoot you and leave you behind for dead. Ready?"

SIXTEEN

Days later, when Clint rode into the North Texas town of Windspring, he noticed the suspicious looks he was getting from the townspeople. Men stared openly at him, while women shied away and hunched their shoulders.

He reined in his horse in front of a saloon with a sign over the door that said, BULL'S HORN SALOON. Across the street was a café called the Trail Dust. He was both hungry and thirsty, so he had a choice to make. Before he could make it, a voice said, "Just stand fast and don't move."

Clint froze.

"You got a gun pointed at me?" he asked.

"I do."

"You intend to shoot me in the back?"

"I do not," the voice said. "I'm the sheriff of this town. I don't make a habit of shooting men in the back."

"Then what's this about?"

"I just wanna have a talk in my office," the man said. "You come along quiet like and we won't have no trouble."

"Well, Sheriff, I'll tell you what. You put your gun away and let me turn around so I can see your badge, and I'll come along quietly."

"I gotta take your gun, mister."

"That's where we're going to have a problem, Sheriff," Clint said. "I don't intend to give up my gun."

"Look, friend—"

"We're not friends, Sheriff," Clint said. "We don't even know each other, but I'm willing to come to your office and talk. I'm just not giving up my gun."

After a moment the sheriff said, "Okay, keep your hands away from your gun and turn around."

Clint turned, holding his hands away from his body. He saw a rather rotund man in his forties wearing a sheriff's badge.

"My name is Sheriff Willis," he said. "Who are you?"

"My name is Clint Adams."

The sheriff froze.

"The Gunsmith?"

"That's right."

"Can you prove it?"

"I've got some telegrams and letters in my saddlebags."

"Jesus . . . you ain't a bank robber."

"I've never been accused of that, no. What's going on, Sheriff?"

Very deliberately, the sheriff holstered his gun.

"Let's go to my office and I'll tell you."

When they got to the office, Willis removed his hat, revealing a bald head with a fringe of hair around it.

"Would you like some coffee?"

"That'd be good. Just black is good."

The lawman poured two cups, handed Clint one, then sat behind his desk. He didn't look comfortable.

"We just had a pretty bad bank robbery in town," he told Clint.

"When did it happen?"

"About a week ago."

"How many men?"

"We're not sure," Willis said. "Seven, eight . . . maybe nine."

"How bad was it?"

"A couple of tellers were killed," he said. "I've only been sheriff since that time, because they killed both our sheriff and his deputy, too."

"Do you know who they were?"

"Strangers, that's all we know," Willis said. "A bunch of strangers rode in, hung around a few days, ate, drank, used the whorehouse, and then all of a sudden one morning they hit the bank."

It sounded like Donovan's method to Clint. He rode in with his crew and they made themselves comfortable, instead of riding in just to hit the bank.

"When I heard another stranger rode into town, I may have overreacted by drawing my gun on you."

"That's okay," Clint said. "I understand."

"I'm not an experienced lawman," Willis said. "I'm a lawyer by trade, but somebody had to step up and wear the badge until the town can find a new sheriff."

"Did a posse go out and look for these bank robbers?" Clint asked.

"There was nobody to put a posse together," Willis said. "Nobody to lead it."

"So it's just a write-off?" Clint asked. "The town loses its money?"

"The town council has been meeting every day to try to hire someone to take a posse out. They haven't had any luck yet."

"Why don't you do it?"

"Like I said," Willis answered, "I'm a lawyer, not a lawman."

"Have you ever ridden in a posse?"

"Well, yes . . ."

"Then you should be able to figure out how to run one," Clint said.

Willis wiped his hand over his face and said, "Yes, maybe you're right . . ."

"How much did they get?"

"Fifty thousand."

"That's a lot."

"I know," Willis said. "The town is devastated."

"Well," Clint said, putting his coffee mug down on the desk, "I hope you figure it out."

"Wait," Willis said as Clint walked to the door.

"What?"

"Why are you in town?"

"I'm looking for a man," Clint said. "He might be riding with those outlaws."

"So you're hunting them?"

"No," Clint said, "I'm just looking for one man. I have to take him home to his kids."

Willis opened his mouth to say something else, but Clint turned and left the office.

SEVENTEEN

The sheriff said the gang ate, drank, and used whores. Clint decided to check the saloons, cafés, and whorehouse to see if one of the gang might have had a big mouth and said where they were going. Also, maybe somebody heard Jimmy McCall's name, which would tell Clint that he was on the right track.

From the sheriff's office, he went back to the Bull's Horn Saloon and ordered himself a beer. The place was only about half full, but he felt the eyes of all the other men trained on him.

The bartender set a mug of beer down in front of him and openly stared. He was in his fifties, a big, rough-hewn man with dark black stubble. He looked like he was spoiling for a fight, but maybe all the men were, given what had happened at their bank.

"I'm looking for a man who might have been riding with the bank robbers who were here last week," Clint said.

"You huntin' them?" the bartender asked.

"No, I'm just looking for one man," Clint said. "His name is Jimmy McCall. Did you hear that name at all while they were here?"

"Tell you the truth," the bartender said, "thinkin' back, seems to me they didn't really call each other by name. Guess I know why now."

"I guess so," Clint said. If they were that careful, he might have a hard time finding something out. He finished his beer, said, "Thanks," and left.

He went directly across the street to the café, got himself seated, and ordered a steak. It was between lunch and supper, so there were only a few folks in the place. When the waiter brought his food, he repeated the same questions he'd asked the bartender.

"Jimmy?" the waiter said, thinking back. "Can't say I heard any of them mention a name. We got some Jimmys in town, but no Jimmy McCall."

"I see," Clint said. "Okay, then, thanks a lot."

"Let me know if you need anything else, mister," the waiter said.

What Clint needed was a sharper knife to cut the steak with, but he made do with what he had, paid his bill, and left.

EIGHTEEN

After he finished eating, he tried a couple of other saloons, but the bartenders there had the same story. Although some of the gang may have drunk there, they never seemed to call each other by name. Clint figured Donovan either had them well trained, or scared enough of him.

As it started to get dark, he decided to check in at the whorehouse.

It wasn't hard to find. There were girls in scanty robes or dresses on the second-level balcony of a two-story house at the south end of town. They waved and called to men as they passed, even showed a breast or a thigh.

Clint stepped to the front door and knocked. The door was answered by a big man in his thirties. He had wide shoulders, bulging arms, and a hard look, which he trained on Clint.

"Whataya want?" he asked.

"I want to talk to someone."

"Ya wanna talk, go to a saloon," the big man said. "We don't supply talk here."

"Okay, then," Clint said, "I'll take whatever you do supply here."

"You got money?"

Clint showed the man some money, offered him some.

"Is there an entry fee?" he asked.

"Naw," the man said, "just go in."

"Thanks."

"If you cause trouble," the man said, "you'll see me again."

"I'll remember that."

Clint went in, found himself in an entry foyer. From there he could see a sitting room filled with men and girls, drinking and talking. There was a stairway to the second floor, and up there he could see men and girls walking together, probably to a room.

Eventually, an older woman in a blue dress with powder applied heavily to her lined face approached him. She was showing cleavage which at one time had probably been impressive, but now it was also powdered and wrinkled.

"Help you, cowboy?" she asked. "Val is my name."

"Well, Val," Clint said, "I'm actually here to talk to some of your girls."

"Talk? That all you want? You can get it a lot cheaper at a saloon."

"That's what your man told me," Clint said. "No, I'm actually looking for a man, and I understand he might have spent some time here."

"Well, you'll have to pay for their time," Val said.

"I'm willing to do that."

"And while you're with them," she said, "you can pay for whatever else you want."

"I'll remember that."

"Well, go on into the parlor," she said. "Choose the girl you want, but you'll have to ask your questions in her room."

"Okay."

"Have a drink if you want," she added. "First one's on the house."

"Thanks."

He went into the parlor. The girls turned their eyes to him, as he was the new meat in the room. The other men frowned at him, tried to get the attention of the women back on them, but Clint was the kind of man who drew attention wherever he went. He figured to use that to his advantage.

"Well, hello," one girl said, approaching him. "What's your name?"

"Clint."

"I'm Angie," she said. "I haven't seen you here before."

"That's because I just got to town today."

"And you came right here lookin' for me?" she asked. "I'm touched."

She was a young redhead, maybe twenty-five, stunning in a green gown that brought out the green of her eyes. The plunging neckline exposed most of her freckled breasts, which were average size, but pushed together to enhance them.

"What can I do for you?" she asked.

"Actually, I need to ask some questions," he said, "but I understand I can't do it down here."

"That's right," she said. "All we can do down here is the dance."

"The dance?"

"Yeah, you know, dance around each other, flirt, feel each other out, and decide if we want to go upstairs."

"You mean, if a man wants to take you upstairs, you don't have to go?"

"We don't have to go with anyone we're not comfortable with."

"That sounds like a good policy."

She moved closer to him so that he could actually feel the heat her body was giving off.

"I feel pretty comfortable with you, though," she said. "How about you?"

"I'm comfortable."

"Wanna go upstairs?"

"Lead the way."

She did. He followed her upstairs, enjoying the way her bottom moved beneath the cloth of her green dress.

On the second floor she walked next to him, her arm linked in his.

"I'm so glad I don't have to come up here with some sweaty, dirty cowboy."

"Well," he said, "I did ride in today. I might not be the cleanest I could be."

"We can fix that," she said. "We got bathtubs here. Just cost a little extra."

"You know," he said, "a bath doesn't sound like a bad idea."

"And I can wash you."

Clint didn't usually pay for sex, but if a bath came

with it, he could just figure that he paid for the bath—
and whatever information he got.

"Sounds good to me, Angie," he said.

"Come on, then," she said. "I'll put you in my room,
and then come and get you when the bath is ready."

NINETEEN

Clint sat in the large tub of hot water while Angie washed him with soap and a cloth. She rubbed his chest, his shoulders, his back, then went to work on his legs and his feet. Finally, she reached into the water for his cock, which was already stiff.

"My, my," she said, "look what we have here."

"I'm only human, you know."

"I can see that," she said. "Well, I'll take good care of it."

She rubbed the soap between her hands until she had a good lather going, then picked up his cock and started cleaning it, stroking it between her soapy fingers. As she continued to stroke him up and down with one hand, she reached deep into the water to wash his testicles with the other.

"We're going to have us an accident here if you're not careful," he warned her.

"Don't worry," she said. "I won't let that happen."

She lovingly kept his hard dick soaped up with one hand, while squeezing it at the base with the other. Whenever he thought he was going to spurt into the water, she stopped him. It was extremely intense.

"You said you had some questions to ask," she said. "Why don't you ask them?"

"Jesus," he said, "how do you expect me to concentrate when you're doing that?"

"Oh? Does this distract you?"

"You know it does."

"I can stop," she offered.

"Not right now you won't."

He reached out and pulled her into the tub with him. She did not resist or object. In fact, she laughed. Once in the water, she removed her flimsy robe and dropped it outside.

She sat between his legs, grabbing his cock again with both hands. He reached out to touch her breasts. They were firm and round, with dark nipples. He rubbed his thumbs over them, then pulled her to him so he could kiss her. He knew many whores didn't kiss, but she did not resist. She opened her mouth, thrust her tongue into his, and moaned. She inched close to him, spreading her legs so that the head of his cock pressed against her vagina.

"Mmm," she said, reaching down to rub the spongy head of his penis along her slit.

"We can't do this in here," he said, lifting her breast to his mouth.

"No," she said, "we'll go back down the hall to my room, now that we are both clean."

She stood in the tub. The water ran down over the

globes of her breasts, dripped from her nipples, and from the red hair between her legs. Clint put his hands around to cup her ass, pulled her crotch into his face. He breathed her in, then extended his tongue to touch her. She jumped, then put her hands on the back of his head as he continued to lick her.

"Oh my God," she said, "I have to lie down if you're gonna do that."

"All right," he said, giving her one last lick and then a slap on the butt. "Out!"

She stepped from the tub, wrapped herself in a towel. Then she held another towel open while he stepped out, and wrapped him in it from the waist down.

"Let's go," she said.

"Walk down the hall like this?" he asked.

"It's all right," she said. "Everyone does it. Come on."

TWENTY

Donovan, McCall, and all but one of the men sat around the campfire, drinking coffee and waiting to eat. One man had been left up the trail, on watch. At the first sign of trouble—namely, a posse—he would fire a shot and the light out himself.

"We got all this money," a man named Long said, "and we're eatin' beans?"

"Just shut up and eat," Donovan said.

They passed around tin plates of beans and then the gang moved away from the fire, leaving Donovan, McCall, and Henry Carter.

"That was a good haul," Carter said. "Better than we thought."

"Yeah," Donovan said, "way better. Good job finding that one, Jimmy."

"Yeah."

Carter looked across the fire at his boss.

"Are we done with them yet?" he asked, jerking his

head to indicate the other four men who were eating.
The gesture also took in the man who was on watch.

"Not yet," Donovan said around a mouthful of beans.
"Go keep an eye and ear on them, though, Henry. Make
sure they ain't thinkin' about bein' done with us."

Carter nodded, carried his plate and cup over to the
other men.

"What about you?" Donovan asked.

"What about me?"

"Why don't you ever complain about eatin' beans all
the time?"

"Maybe it's because I remember a time when me and
my family didn't even have beans," Jimmy said.

"Well, those times are gonna be done pretty soon,
Jimmy."

"How soon?"

"Don't be impatient," Donovan said. "We still got
lots of money to make together."

"Sure," McCall said. "That's what it's all about,
right? Money?"

"That's *all* it's about, Jimmy. That's the only thing.
Money."

That gave McCall an odd sense of calm. As long as
he was worth money to Donovan, there was no way the
man was going to turn on him and kill him.

Not yet anyway.

Later, Donovan settled down into his sleeping bag for
a nap. There was plenty of daylight left, and the other
men were wondering why they weren't on the move.

"If the posse is on our trail—" Long started, but
Jimmy McCall cut him off.

"There's no posse."

"How can you be sure?" Long asked.

Carter and McCall were again hunkered around the fire, this time with the other men. Donovan's absence brought them all to the fire.

"We—you killed the sheriff and the deputy," McCall said. "It'll be a while before they can hire new ones. By that time we'll be in Mexico." He looked over at Donovan's sleeping form. "If that's where he's takin' us."

Long, who seemed to be the spokesman for the others, looked at Carter.

"Where *is* he takin' us?"

"Only he knows that," Carter said.

"Well, why don't you ask 'im?"

Carter looked at Long and replied, "Why don't you ask 'im?"

Long looked around, then muttered, "I ain't gonna question 'im."

He turned and walked away from the fire. The other men followed him.

Carter looked at McCall.

"You sure about the law in that town?"

"A sheriff and one deputy," McCall said. "I'm sure. And they're dead."

"Well, we still should be movin'," Carter said.

"Tell him," McCall said, jerking his head toward the sleeping Donovan.

"I'm with Long on that," Carter said. "I ain't about to start questionin' Donovan."

"Well then," McCall said, "I guess we'll just have to keep waitin' for him to tell us somethin'."

Carter looked over at Donovan again.

"What are you thinkin'?" McCall asked.

Carter looked at McCall, seemed to be considering something, but then shook his head and said, "Nothin'. I ain't thinkin' nothin'."

He poured himself a cup of coffee, then turned and walked away from the fire. He didn't, however, join the other men. He remained on his own.

TWENTY-ONE

Clint followed Angie down the hall. Another man ran past, naked, chasing a naked girl, both of them laughing. Neither of them seemed to notice either Clint or Angie.

When they got to her room, she opened the door and let him go in first, then stepped in and closed the door. She also locked it. He set his clothes aside, made sure the gun was within easy reach of the door.

"I don't wanna be disturbed," she said.

He sat down on the bed.

She stood in front of him and removed her towel.

"Still wanna ask questions?"

"Don't want to," he said. "I have to."

She frowned at him, then put her hands on her hips and said, "Okay, go ahead."

"You mind putting your towel back on?" he asked. "Just for the question-and-answer part?"

"Oh, all right."

She bent over, grabbed the towel, and wrapped it

around herself again, covering her breasts and barely covering her crotch.

"Better?"

"Better."

"Good thing you have yours on."

He looked down at his lap, saw the outline there of his cock, still hard.

"Better ask your questions," she said. "I'm gonna be going for that any minute now."

"Jimmy McCall," he said.

"What about him?"

"You know him?"

She frowned.

"The name sounds familiar."

"He was in town with the gang that robbed the bank," he said.

"Some of them came here for a few days before the robbery," she said. "He was one of them?"

"Yes."

"You know," she said, "those boys never did say their names when they were with us. In fact, I never heard them call each other by name."

"Then why does Jimmy McCall sound familiar?" he asked.

She came over and sat next to him on the bed.

"I don't know," she said. "One of the girls was with a guy named Jimmy. But McCall . . . maybe I just heard that later."

"Could you find out which girl?"

"You want me to go around and ask all the girls?" she asked, looking at him.

"I guess I could do that myself."

"Oh, no," she said, putting her arm on his, "I'm not sharin' you with them. Don't worry, I'll find out which one of them was with Jimmy. Then you can ask her your questions."

"Okay," he said, "that suits me."

She ran her hand over his chest.

"Is that the end of the questions?"

"That's all I have to ask," he said, "for now."

He leaned over and kissed her. Her arms went around his neck, and her towel fell away. He used one hand to cup her right breast, teasing the nipple with his thumb. She moaned, reached down, and loosened the towel around his waist. Then she took his cock into her hand and began to stroke it.

This time he moaned and kissed her more deeply. He squeezed her breast and she gasped, returned the favor by tightening her grip on his penis.

She broke from his hold, then, and slid to the floor on her knees. She took his cock in both hands and guided it into her hot, avid mouth. She began to suck him, sliding her hand up and down the part of the shaft that did not go into her mouth.

Clint leaned back on his hands, began to lift his hips, moving in unison with her sucking motion. This time, she didn't use her technique to keep him from finishing. She sucked him until he exploded into her mouth with a loud groan.

"What'd you do that for?" he asked as she stared up at him with a smile.

"Oh, don't worry," she said. She stood up, pushed him down on his back. "You're far from done. I just wanted to keep you too weak to leave my room."

"What makes you think I want to leave your room?"

She climbed on top of him, started to run her wet pussy up and down the length of his cock. Immediately, he began to stiffen again.

"See?"

"You're going to try to kill me, aren't you?" he asked.

"Oh, no, honey," she said, rubbing her breasts in his face, "I'm gonna do everything I can to keep you alive."

TWENTY-TWO

The members of the town council watched as portly Sheriff Willis entered the room. At the head of the table was Mayor Plummer.

"All right," Plummer, a rotund man in his own right, said. "Sheriff Willis called this meeting, so let's hear what he has to say."

"Like I told you when I accepted this job, I'm a law-*yer*, not a law*man*. You fellas were supposed to find somebody to replace me."

"We been trying, Louis," Plummer said. "We just haven't had any luck."

"Well, a man rode into town today who I think will change your luck."

"Is that a fact?" Plummer asked, looking around at the other men. "And who is that?"

"Clint Adams."

One of the other men at the table said, "The Gunsmith is in our town?"

"He is," Willis said, "and that's not the best part."

"What's the best part, Louis?" Plummer asked. "Please, don't keep us in suspense."

"He's already looking for one of the members of the gang."

"Do you think he'd accept the badge?" Plummer asked.

"Not for what you're paying your sheriffs," Willis said. "You'll have to commit a lot more money to the job if you want him to take it."

"For Chrissake," one of the board members said, "our bank was robbed."

"Well," Willis said, "he's not going to do it for the fun of it."

"You said he's already looking for one of the gang members," Plummer said. "Why don't we just let him do it?"

"Because when he catches up to them, that's all he'll do," Willis said. "He won't bring the gang to justice, or bring the money back. For that, you'll have to pay him."

"Did you talk to him?" the mayor asked.

"I did."

"Do you know how much he's going to want?" Plummer asked.

"I didn't talk to him about that," Willis said. "I didn't bring it up."

"Why not?" a board member asked.

"I was just questioning him as a stranger in town," Willis said. "When I found out who he was, I let him walk."

"Is he even still in town?" Plummer asked.

"Yes, he is. He's asking questions, trying to find out if any of the gang members said anything that would tell where they went."

"Who would they have been stupid enough to tell that to?" another man asked.

Willis shrugged. "A bartender? A whore? That's what he's trying to find out."

"All right," Plummer said.

"All right . . . you'll do it?" Willis asked.

"We have to vote," a board member objected.

"Vote on what, Sam?" Plummer asked. "On whether or not we want our money back?" He looked at Willis. "Give me the badge, Louis, if you don't mind."

"I don't mind at all." Willis stepped forward, took the badge from his chest, and set it down on the table. A great weight seemed to lift from his shoulders.

"Now can you ask Mr. Adams to come and see me?" Plummer asked.

"Yes, sir," Willis said. "I'll find him and ask him."

"Then this meeting's adjourned," Plummer said. "Louis, will you stay a moment?"

"Sure."

The other members of the board stood and filed out of the room. Not all of them were completely happy.

Finally, the room was empty but for Willis and the mayor.

"It must be a great relief, Willis, to get that target off your chest."

"You have no idea," Willis said. "I just took the job because we're friends, Mr. Mayor. It was a favor to you, Jackson."

"Well, I'm going to ask you for another favor, Louis," the mayor said.

"What's that, Jackson?"

"I want you to go with Adams."

"What?"

"We need someone from this town to go with him," the mayor said. "What if he catches them and decides to keep the money?"

"First," Willis said, "how do you expect me to spend days on the back of a horse? Second, he hasn't even taken the job yet. Why don't we wait and see what happens?"

"No," Plummer said, "I want you to be in my office when I talk to him, when I offer him the job."

"You think my presence will make him take the job?" Willis asked. "And you think my presence on the trail with him will keep him from taking the money? Jesus, Jackson, he'll just kill me and take it."

"There is nothing in the man's reputation to indicate he's a thief or a murderer."

"No, not a murderer," Willis said. "Just a killer."

"Louis," Plummer said, "I can't trust anyone else to do this."

"Why don't you do it yourself?"

"I would," Plummer said, "but with my bum leg, I'd never be able to sit a horse for that long." He touched his leg, which had atrophied from an earlier injury.

"Damn you," Willis said, because he knew the man's reason was real.

"You'll do it?"

"I'll be in your office when you offer him the job." Willis said. "Let's just get there."

"All right," Plummer said. "Then go and get him, Louis."

"I'll have to find him first."

"That shouldn't be too hard," Plummer said. "From what you said, he's either in a saloon, or the whorehouse."

TWENTY-THREE

The door opened and Angie came back in, wearing her robe. Clint was lying on his back in her bed, still naked.

"It was Sue Min," she said.

"What?"

She came over and sat next to him on the bed.

"It was Sue Min," she said again. "She was with a man named Jimmy during that week."

"Will she talk to me?" he asked.

"She will," Angie said. Absently, she reached out and stroked his cock. "When I'm done with you."

"You're not done with me?"

She gripped his cock and it swelled in her hand.

"What do you think?"

He looked down at his stiffening cock and said, "I guess not."

"Yeah, you bet not."

She stood up, discarded her robe, then got back on the bed with him. Spreading his legs wide, she settled down between them, lying on her belly, and took his cock into her mouth . . .

Later, Angie walked Clint—now fully dressed, but weak in the legs—to Sue Min's room.

"Ten minutes," Angie said. "Then she has to go back to work."

"Okay."

"And don't get yourself trapped by her," Angie said. "She's kinda pretty."

"Okay."

"Good luck," she said. "Come say good-bye before you leave."

"I will."

He knocked on the door and entered.

Downstairs the ex-Sheriff Willis entered and asked the madame if Clint Adams was in the place.

"Louis, you know I don't ask names," she said.

"He's tall, kinda rough looking, a little dusty. Says he's looking for a fella, one of the gang members."

"Oh, him," she said. "Yeah, he's upstairs with Angie. Said he wanted to talk to the girls, but he's been with her for a while. Maybe he's doin' more than talkin'."

"Thanks, Val."

He started for the stairs, but Val blocked his way.

"What's the matter with you, Louis? You know you can't go there."

"Val, I need to talk to him."

"Well, take a girl upstairs, or wait for him to come down."

"If I take a girl upstairs, my wife'll kill me."

"Then I guess you'll be waiting for him to come down," she said. "Have a seat in the parlor. I'll have one of the girls bring you a drink."

"Okay, Val," he said. "Have it your way."

He went into the parlor and was immediately besieged by girls.

Clint entered the room and closed the door. The girl curled up on the bed was Oriental, and petite. She had long, straight black hair, and a bloodred mouth. She was wearing a silk robe that hugged her doll-like body.

"You are Clint?" she asked.

"I am."

"You are asking questions about Jimmy McCall?"

"I am."

"Why do you want him?"

"His children miss him," Clint said. "I'm supposed to take him home to them."

She smiled.

"He talked to me about them," she said. "He loves them very much, and he misses them."

"Did he tell you where he'd be going after the gang left here?"

"He said he did not know where they would go," she answered. "He said he had to stay with them until the leader—Donovan?—split the money. Split? Is that correct?"

"Yes, that's correct."

"This does not help you?"

He hesitated, then said, "No, it helps a little. At least I know he wants to see his children."

"Oh, yes," she said, "he does."

"What about a direction?" he asked. If he rode around the entire town, he'd eventually find the trail left by the gang, but if he knew what direction they were going, it would save him time. "Did he give any indication of what direction they might be going in?"

She studied Clint for a few moments, then asked, "You do not want to kill him?"

"No," he said, "I don't want to kill him. I promise you."

"I believe you," she said. "South. He said he thought they would be going south. Possibly Mexico."

"Thank you, Sue Min," he said. "Thank you a lot."

"You are welcome."

He turned and reached for the doorknob.

"You do not wish to stay?" she asked.

He turned to look at her and stopped short when he realized she had shrugged the robe from her shoulders. Her breasts were small, perfectly formed, with dark, hard nipples.

"I could make you feel very nice," she said, rubbing one of her breasts with a small hand.

"I'm sure you could," he said, "but I simply don't have the time."

He left, not bothering to mention that her doll-like body held no allure for him. In fact, he found it very odd. He preferred women with more meat on them.

In the hall he knocked on Angie's door to say good-bye, before going downstairs.

TWENTY-FOUR

When Clint Adams came down the stairs, Lou Willis pulled himself away from the girls in the parlor to intercept him before he left.

"Mr. Adams."

"Sheriff," Clint said. "Is this a coincidence? In the middle of the afternoon?"

"What? No, no, I'm a married man."

"Then you're here looking for me?"

"Yes, I am," Willis said. "Did you get the information you were looking for?"

"I did, actually," Clint said. "I was just about to get going."

"I wonder if we can have a moment of your time?" Willis asked.

"We?"

"Yes, the mayor—Mayor Plummer—would like to talk to you."

Clint had a feeling this was about the money. Perhaps the mayor wanted him to bring the money back.

"It won't take long," Willis promised.

"All right," Clint said. "Okay, let's go. Lead the way."

Willis led Clint to City Hall, and up a flight of steps to the mayor's office. Along the way he chattered, talking incessantly, but saying very little.

Willis opened the door to the office and let Clint enter first. The fat man behind the desk stood up immediately.

"Clint Adams, this is Mayor Jackson Plummer," Willis said.

"Mr. Adams," Plummer said, extending his hand.

Clint crossed the room and shook the man's pudgy hand.

"Mr. Mayor."

"Won't you sit down?"

"Thank you."

"Can I get you something to drink?" the politician asked.

"No, after this I'll be getting myself something to eat before I leave town."

"Ah, you're leaving today?" the mayor asked, seating himself.

"Yes, sir."

"Then you must have gotten the information you were looking for."

"Not exactly," Clint said, "but I found out something helpful."

"And what was that?"

"One of the girls gave me a possible direction the gang may have gone in."

"Oh, well, that's good. You're probably wondering why I asked Willis to bring you here."

"Let's cut to the chase, Mayor," Clint said. "You want me to recover your money, if I can. I have to tell you I'm only going after one man, not the whole gang."

"That is what I wanted to talk to you about, Mr. Adams. We don't have a proper sheriff. I'd like to offer you the job." He took the badge—last seen on the chest of Willis—out of a drawer and tossed it on the desk.

"You fired Mr. Willis?"

"Mr. Willis gave the badge up," Plummer said. "His position was only temporary."

"Well, Mayor, I can't take the job. I'm going to find my man and take him back to his kids in New Mexico. I can't be your town sheriff."

"We don't want you to keep the job," Plummer said. "Just wear the badge while you chase down the gang. It will give you some kind of authority."

Clint eyed the badge. A little authority might not hurt for what he had to do.

"We can give you some men," Plummer said.

"How long would it take you to assemble a posse?"

"Well," Plummer said, "now that you'd be leading it, we'd just have to get the word out . . . a few days?"

"That's too long," Clint said.

"We're not a town of men who are used to wearing guns and riding the trail for extended periods of time," Plummer said.

"I tell you what," Clint said. "I'll take your badge

with me, put it to good use, and then bring it back with the money—if I can." Clint leaned forward to grab the tin from the desk.

"I have a favor to ask, before you pick up the badge," Plummer said.

Clint stopped his motion.

"What's that?"

"Take Willis with you."

Clint turned and looked at Willis, who shrugged sheepishly.

"Why him?"

"I think we need someone along with you to represent the town's interests."

"You think I might take the money for myself?"

"Not at all."

"But I might."

"Well, you might."

"And having Willis along would stop me?"

"Look, Mr. Adams, I don't really think—"

"Hey," Clint said, "if he wants to come, he can come. But he'll have to keep up."

"We'll give him the best horse in town," Plummer said.

Clint leaned forward and plucked the badge off the desk. He dropped it into his shirt pocket.

"You're not going to wear it?" Plummer asked.

"I said I'd take it with me," Clint said. "I didn't say I'd wear it."

He stood up, and the mayor followed. They shook hands.

"That meal? If you want a good steak, go to the Versailles Café. Best place in town."

"Thank you."

"Still leaving today? Why not wait 'til morning?"

"They have a big head start," Clint said. "I don't want it to get any bigger."

"Well then," Plummer said, "good luck, and thanks."

"Thank me when I bring the money back." He turned to Willis. "Come on, Willis. I'll buy you a steak."

"No, no," Plummer said, "the steak is on the town. Arrange it, Willis."

"I will."

"Then once again, Willis," Clint said, "lead the way."

Outside, on the boardwalk, Clint asked, "Was your coming along his idea or yours?"

"His," Willis said.

"How did he talk you into it?"

"He appealed to my sense of civic duty."

"How long will it take you to get yourself together?" Clint asked.

"After the steak? An hour."

"Good, that'll leave us a couple hours of daylight left to pick up the trail. Then we can camp and start tracking them in earnest tomorrow."

They started walking.

"Can you shoot?" Clint asked.

"I'm pretty good with a rifle."

"Good. Once we clear the town, though, you'll have to show me. I've got be sure just how much I can depend on you."

"No problem," Willis said. He wished.

TWENTY-FIVE

Clint didn't know if the Versailles was the best place in town, but the mayor was right about one thing: they served a good steak. Surrounded by all the trimmings, and accompanied by a basket of biscuits, it was certainly the best free meal Clint had had in some time. Washing it down with beer made it that much better.

After the meal, Clint had a piece of peach pie, while Willis had apple. The waiter knew Willis well, so he brought them each a second piece.

"I feel bad, taking this for free," Clint said. "I should pay—"

"Don't worry," the waiter said. "I'll get paid by the city."

"This is your place?"

"Cook and waiter. Sweep up after I close, too."

The man went back to the kitchen. Clint glanced around. There were only six sets of sturdy tables and chairs, all of which looked handmade.

"You sure about this, Mr. Willis?" Clint asked.

"Lou," Willis said, "my name's Lou. And you mean about going with you? Yeah, I'm sure."

"Then we better go and get you that horse," Clint said.

"The mayor said they'd give me the best one in town."

"And who's to say which one is the best?" Clint asked. "I'll come along and help pick it out."

"Fine by me."

"Then we'll pick up a few things and hit the road."

"Might as well get going, then."

They stood up, Willis squared the bill with the waiter/owner—City Hall would send over the money—and they walked to the livery.

The liveryman took them out back, where there was a corral filled with horses.

"Sure doesn't look like a posse would have trouble getting horses," Clint said.

"Posse?" the old liveryman said. "In this town? Take you days to get one up. These folks around here don't know nothin' about ridin' or shootin'. That's why them bank robbers is gettin' away with the town's money."

"What about that one?" Willis asked, pointing.

"No," Clint said, "you're going to need something that can keep up with mine."

Willis stayed outside while Clint went into the corral to have a look. He found an able-bodied, rangy sorrel who'd have a long strike, might be able to keep up with Eclipse.

"That one," he told the liveryman, "and a saddle."

"Yes, sir."

"The city's paying, Al," Willis said.

"What? Top price?"

"Yeah, yeah, Al," Willis said, "you'll get top price."

"Yeah, we'll see," the old man said. "I'll saddle him up and bring 'im out front to you."

"We'll meet you there," Clint said.

When they collected the horse, they walked both their animals to the mercantile, picked up some coffee, beans, beef jerky, and a few cans of peaches. This was stuff Clint knew he could carry easily. They split it up between their saddlebags and rode out of town.

TWENTY-SIX

They rode south and picked up the trail.

"See here?" Clint said, pointing at the ground. "Seven, maybe eight horses."

"How can you tell?"

"The tracks are that different," he said. "Each horse has its own pattern, its own signature."

"I don't see it," Willis admitted.

"Luckily, I do. Let's mount up,"

They got back on the horses and followed the tracks south until it started to get dark. Then they camped.

"Geez, my ass is sore," Willis said as they sat around the fire and ate beans. "It's been years since I was on a horse this long."

"It'll feel better tomorrow," Clint said. "You just have to get used to it again."

"How far south do you intend to chase this gang?" Willis asked.

"Mexico, if I have to."

"Can we do that?" Willis asked. "Go into Mexico after them?"

"Sure."

"With authority?"

"Well . . . no, not with authority."

"Then what rights will we have once we cross?"

"We'll have right on our side, Lou," Clint said. "And if we run into the *rurales*, maybe we can get them to back us."

"And if not?"

"I'll think about that when we get there," Clint said. He looked across the fire at the lawyer. "Lou, you can turn back anytime you want."

"No, I can't," Willis said. "I'm representing the town, remember?"

"Okay, then," Clint said. "We'll set a watch. I'll go first, wake you in four hours."

"Why are we on watch?" Willis asked. "We're chasing them."

"Just in case."

"Just in case . . . what?"

Clint shrugged.

"They could double back," he said. "They could split their take and some of them might come back this way. Who knows?"

"W-What do I watch for?"

"Just listen," Clint said. "The horses will alert you if somebody's coming. If they do, wake me up."

"What if I wake you up for nothing?"

"Better than me not waking up at all," Clint said. "Go ahead, Lou. You get some sleep."

"I don't know if I can sleep on the ground," Willis said, "but I'll try."

"Don't worry," Clint said. "You're tired enough."

Willis wrapped himself in his bedroll, and in a matter of minutes, he was asleep.

In another camp two fires were going. Around one sat Andy Donovan, Jimmy McCall, and Henry Carter. Around the other sat the rest of the men.

"Tomorrow we'll be in Mexico," Donovan said.

"You think the boys are gonna go that far?" Carter asked. "Mexico?"

"If they want their share of the money, they will," Donovan said.

Carter looked at McCall, who had nothing to say.

"What about you?" he asked. "Are you doin' to Mexico?"

Jimmy looked at Carter and said, "If Donovan's goin' to Mexico, that's where I'm goin'."

Carter took his beans and walked to the other fire.

"Do you know what he's doin' over there?" Jimmy asked Donovan.

"Yeah, he's doin' what I tell him to do," the gang leader said. "He's keepin' an eye on those guys, findin' out what's on their minds."

"And what do you think is on his mind?"

"What are you gettin' at?"

"You're afraid those men might turn on you sometime, huh?" Jimmy asked.

"I keep my eye on them."

"And what about Henry?"

"What about him?"

"You trust him?"

"Jimmy, you know me. You know I don't trust anybody—not even you."

"Well, if I was you, I'd keep an eye on all of them," Jimmy said. "Even Henry. Maybe especially Henry."

Donovan poured himself some more coffee, picked up his plate to finish his beans. Then he turned his head and looked over to where Carter was talking with the other men.

"Jimmy."

"Yeah?"

"You wanna go home to your kids?"

"You know I do."

"Keep me alive long enough to split the money, and you'll be rich."

"Tell me somethin'."

"What?"

"You intend to split this money with them at all?"

"Probably not."

"So you need to turn on them before they turn on you," Jimmy said.

"I intend to."

"Then why not now?"

"I'm not ready now."

"Mexico?"

"I'll probably be ready there. And I'll need you to help me."

"It would be good if you had Carter, too."

"We'll see," Donovan said. "But you and me, we can handle them if we have to."

"How much money do we have, Andy?" Jimmy asked.

"Almost enough," Donovan said, "almost enough."

TWENTY-SEVEN

Three days out from Windspring, Clint woke up to the smell of fresh coffee.

"You made a pot?" he asked, rolling out of his bedroll.

"I thought I might try pulling my weight," Willis said. "Want some jerky?"

"Sure."

Willis handed him a piece of jerk, and then a cup of coffee. He watched while Clint sipped it.

"How is it?"

"Not bad," Clint said. "Not bad at all. You're learning."

"You said you liked it strong," Willis said. "It almost ate through the bottom of the pot."

Clint laughed and said, "That's strong, all right."

Willis smiled, sipped, and winced, then they both laughed.

"How far out are we from Mexico?"

"A couple of days."

"And how far behind the gang are we?"

"Three days, maybe more," Clint said. "By my reckoning, they're already in Mexico."

"And we're definitely crossing after them?"

"I am," Clint said. "I don't know about you."

"Oh, if you're going, I'm going, too," Willis said.

"Then let's finish this elaborate breakfast and get going."

Donovan and his gang stopped at a small village called San Angel. Little more than a collection of adobe buildings housing a cantina, a small hotel, and a church.

"You boys go ahead and get something to drink or eat," Donovan said, "or both. Aikens, you and Booth take the horses to the stables. Don't unsaddle them. We won't be stayin'."

"Okay, boss."

"And don't nobody get drunk," Donovan said. "Jimmy, you come with me."

"Okay."

McCall gave the reins of his horse to Aikens, then followed Donovan on foot.

"Where are we goin'?" Jimmy asked.

"The hotel."

"I thought we weren't stayin'."

"We're not."

"Then why are we goin' to the hotel?"

"To meet somebody."

"Who?"

"You'll see."

* * *

Henry Carter went into the cantina with four of the other men, including Long.

They bellied up to the bar and ordered tequila or beer, then asked the bartender for some tacos.

"*Sí, señor,*" he said. "*Immediatamente!*"

Long and Carter moved to one end of the bar, where the others couldn't hear them.

"So what do you think?" Long asked.

"Not yet," Carter said. "Not here. We don't have all the men yet."

"We have enough," Long said.

"No," Carter said, "we need them all."

"There's just Billings and Dade."

"We need them. That'll just leave Donovan with Jimmy McCall to back him."

"You can't get McCall over to our side?"

"I doubt it," Carter said. "I'll feel him out, but I doubt it. I think we're gonna have to kill him, too. A shame."

"Why?"

"All he wants to do is get back to his kids."

"So tell him if we kill Donovan, he can go see his kids. Hell, we'll all go see his kids."

"Yeah, okay," Carter said. "For now let's just eat and drink before Donovan comes in here and yells at us to mount up."

"Why isn't he in here eatin'?"

"I don't know," Carter said. "I'm not gonna worry about that now."

They moved down the bar to join the other men eating tacos and washing them down with beer and tequila.

* * *

When they entered the hotel, the desk clerk had his head down on the desk, snoring.

Donovan walked to the desk and slapped his hand down on it. The clerk jerked his head up, eyes wide.

"Sí, señor?" he said. "Do you need a room?"

"I'm looking for a man named Rodrigo."

"Rodrigo?"

"Yes."

"I do not know—"

Donovan drew his gun and pointed it at the man, whose eyes went wide.

"Let's try again."

"Sí, señor," the man said. "Rodrigo is in Room 5. He is, uh, with someone."

"That's okay," Donovan said. "We'll just interrupt him."

"Sí, señor."

Donovan holstered his gun.

"You can go back to sleep now."

"Sí, señor. Gracias, señor."

Donovan looked at McCall and said, "Let's go."

"Are we gonna need our guns?"

"No," Donovan said. "Rodrigo is expecting me."

"So he won't mind being interrupted while he's . . . with his guest?"

Donovan laughed.

"Oh, yeah, he'll be mad," he said, "but that's just too damn bad."

TWENTY-EIGHT

When they got to the door of Room 5, they heard sounds from inside, two people grunting and groaning.

"Maybe we should wait," Jimmy McCall said.

"No time," Donovan said. He reached for the doorknob, turned it, found the door unlocked. He slammed it open.

At the sound of the door hitting the wall, the man on the bed leaped off it and went for the gun on the chair next to him.

"Easy, Rodrigo!" Donovan yelled.

Rodrigo stopped and stared at Donovan. When he recognized him, he relaxed and stood up straight, ignoring his gun. He was naked, and aroused.

The girl on the bed was naked, a dark-haired, dark-skinned Mexican woman who was forty if she was a day. She had a body that had once been bountiful, but now sagged. Still, she probably looked good to a man who had spent many days on horseback.

"Cabron!" she said.

Jimmy didn't know if she was cursing Donovan, or Rodrigo.

"We need to talk, Rodrigo."

"Mi amigo, Donovan," Rodrigo said. *"Como esta?"*

"I'm doin' fine, Rodrigo," Donovan said. "Sorry to interrupt you." He walked to the bed, took out some money, and dropped it on the mattress. "There you go, *señorita*. Now git!"

She grabbed at the money, then hopped off the bed and picked her clothes up from the floor. She didn't bother putting them on, just carried them with her as she went out into the hall. McCall closed the door behind her.

"Get dressed, Rodrigo," Donovan said. "Nobody wants to look at your tallywacker."

The Mexican grabbed his pants and pulled them on, covering his wilting penis.

"My friend, it is so good to see you," he said. "Who is this?"

"My *compadre*, Jimmy McCall," Donovan said. "My men are over at the cantina."

"Perhaps we should go there and join them?"

"In a minute," Donovan said. "You got the information I need?"

"Sí, as promised," Rodrigo said.

"Let's have it."

Rodrigo crossed the room, took something out of his saddlebags. As McCall watched, the man unfurled it and he realized it was a map of Mexico. Rodrigo spread it out on the bed.

"C'mere, Jimmy."

Donovan and Jimmy approached the bed. Rodrigo pointed to something on the map.

"This town is called Casa Madera. It is the one you want."

Donovan pointed. "It's kind of close to Mexico City."

"That's why it has so much money, *señor*," Rodrigo said.

"And what about law?"

"That you will have to go in and see for yourself, *señor.*"

"That'll be my man Jimmy's job," Donovan said. "But if they put out the word they been hit, how long before some troops from Mexico City can make it there?"

"You will have two hours, *señor*. Perhaps more."

"Okay, that's good."

Jimmy put his hand on Donovan's arm.

"Two hours is cutting it close."

"Don't worry," Donovan said. "We'll be fine as long as you do your part." He looked at the Mexican. "Let me have that map, Rodrigo. Why don't you go over to the cantina and have a drink on me. We'll be there soon."

"*Sí, señor,*" Rodrigo said. "A drink sounds very good. *Muy bien.*"

Rodrigo put on his shirt and boots and hurried from the room, as if he thought all the tequila would be gone before he got there.

Donovan turned to Jimmy.

"You got questions?"

"Yeah, I got questions," McCall said. "I thought we were coming to Mexico to split the money."

"We are," Donovan said, "but we're gonna get a little more before we do that."

"You want me to scout a Mexican town? I'll stick out like . . . well, a gringo in a Mexican town."

"Don't worry about that," Donovan said. "Mexico is filthy with gringos."

"So this is why you didn't want to get rid of the other men yet," McCall said. "One more job."

"One more," Donovan said, "then you'll have your money and you can go back to your kids."

"Is this on the level, Andy?"

"On the level, Jimmy. Now why don't we go and get somethin' to eat?"

"Yeah," McCall said, "okay."

TWENTY-NINE

Clint and Willis stopped and looked out over the Rio Grande.

"Can we ride across that?" Willis asked. "Looks like it's moving pretty fast."

"We'll find a place to cross," Clint said.

"What about the tracks we were following?"

"We'll pick them up again on the other side," Clint said.

Willis wasn't so sure.

"Will the horses be okay?"

"The horses will be fine," Clint assured him. "Don't worry."

"I can't really swim," Willis said.

"Just stay in the saddle," Clint said, "and the horse will take you across."

"Are you sure?"

"Positive. Just follow me."

Clint gigged his horse and started toward the river.

Willis waited a moment, then followed, still not sure he was going to make it to the other side.

They rode for a few minutes, then Clint turned and said, "We'll cross here."

"If you say so."

"I'll go first," Clint said. "All you have to watch for is anything dangerous coming down the river."

"Dangerous?"

"I mean like a big branch or log," Clint said. "You don't want to get hit by anything."

"But what if—" Willis started, but he stopped when Clint urged Eclipse into the river.

He watched as Clint and Eclipse expertly negotiated the river. He saw what Clint meant about giving the horse his head. Eclipse seemed to know exactly what to do, and there was no flotsam coming down the river, heading for them.

Eventually, Clint got to the other side, turned, and waved to Willis.

Willis gigged his horse forward. The animal stepped gingerly into the water, and Willis wondered if his horse had ever done anything like this before.

They moved into the water, which eventually came up to his knees. Willis kept looking upriver for logs, trees, or maybe a shark. He'd been on a ship once, had seen sharks and, at one point, a whale. Whales were too big for the river, but the Rio Grande would accommodate a shark just fine.

The horse began to cross with authority and Willis felt that he had been concerned for no reason. Yeah, he was more comfortable in a courtroom than on a horse, but this wasn't so bad.

Suddenly, he became aware that Clint was yelling and waving to him. It looked like he was pointing upriver. Willis looked and saw a large tree branch coming toward him. There were branches sticking up from the water, but in the water was a solid chunk of tree.

"Damn it," he said, kicking his horse in the sides to try and get it to go faster. He wished he had spurs on.

The branch kept getting closer, and it seemed to him that he and the horse were just treading water—then suddenly there was ground beneath them, and the horse was taking him onto shore as the tree went by.

Clint rode over to meet him.

"I thought you were going to ride in right after me," he said.

"I decided to watch you do it," Willis said. He hadn't realized how out of breath he was.

"Well, you're lucky that tree missed you," Clint said. "Your horse knew what to do."

Willis opened his mouth to speak, but he still hadn't caught his breath.

"Take a minute and relax," Clint said. "I'm going to check up and down the river for tracks."

Willis dismounted, then his legs went out on him and he found himself sitting on the ground. He held on to his horse's reins, though, so the animal didn't go wandering off.

He tried to breathe.

Clint rode along the river's edge, trying to find tracks left by the gang, but it had been days since they had forded the river.

He moved away from the river's shore a bit, and that

was when he found the tracks. He rode back to Willis, who was sitting on the ground, panting.

"You okay?"

Willis waved.

"I found their tracks," he said. "You up to moving on?"

Willis waved again, staggered to his feet. Clint watched as he struggled to get back into the saddle, but he did it.

"Okay," Clint said, "just follow me."

THIRTY

Donovan and McCall sat in a corner at a table that was covered with *enchiladas*, *frijoles refritos*, and *tortillas*.

"Hey," Donovan called to the waitress, *"mas cervezas!"*

"Sí, señor."

"That's a good-lookin' *señorita*," Donovan said. "Why don't you try your luck?"

"No, thanks," McCall said. "She's all yours."

"I just might," Donovan said, cutting into an *enchilada*.

"You're supposed to pick those up and eat 'em," McCall said.

"What am I, an animal?" Donovan asked.

McCall shook his head, picked up an *enchilada*, and bit into it.

The waitress came over with two more beers and set them down. Donovan slapped her on the ass.

"Yeah," he said as she walked away, "if we wuz stayin' here overnight, I'd give her a ride she wouldn't forget."

McCall nodded, bit into his *enchilada* again.

Across the room, Henry Carter was sitting with Long and two other men. The rest were at the bar. Rodrigo was standing at one end of the bar alone.

"What do you know about this Mex?" Long asked Carter.

"Nothin'," Carter said, "I never heard of 'im."

"Is he gonna be ridin' with us?"

"Looks like it."

"So that's another gun on Donovan's side."

"I guess so."

"Unless we can get him to switch."

"None of us know him," Carter said. "Donovan does. Why would he switch sides?"

"Money?" Long asked. "Lots of people switch sides for money, don't they?"

Carter frowned. Was Long digging at him?

"We'll see," he said. He got up, took his beer, and walked over to where Donovan and McCall were sitting. He sat with them.

"What's with this Mex?" he asked.

"You want somethin' to eat, Henry?" Donovan asked.

"No, I ate," Carter said. "Who's this Mex and why is he gonna ride with us?"

"He's a friend of mine," Donovan said, "and he's ridin' with us because I say so. You got a problem with that?"

"No, no, Andy," Carter said, "I don't have a problem.

Some of the boys was just wonderin' if he was in for a full share."

"He's in for a share of any job we pull while he's with us."

"Are we pullin' a job in Mexico?"

"I'll let you know," Donovan said. "If the men are finished eatin' and drinkin', get them ready to ride. We'll head out as soon as I finish my meal."

"Yeah, okay."

Carter got up and walked over to the men.

"You push him and he'll join them when they turn on you," McCall said.

"He's already joined them," Donovan said. "When the time comes, we're gonna have to kill him, too."

"And what about Rodrigo?"

"He'll fight with us."

"You sure?"

"I am."

McCall washed down his food with a swig of beer.

"So I'm supposed to ride into Casa Madera and take a look at their bank?"

"Take a look at everythin'," Donovan said. "Like you always do. You can head out now, and we'll follow."

McCall regarded Donovan over his half-finished beer.

"You're finished with your meal, right?"

"Yes," McCall said, putting his beer down, "I'm done."

Donovan leaned forward as McCall stood up.

"Remember, Jimmy," Donovan said, "this is your last one. After this you can go home to your kids."

"Yeah," Jimmy McCall said, "if I live that long."

* * *

The first town Clint and Willis came to was Alvarado. The tracks of the gang showed that they'd skirted the town, but Clint decided to stop. Willis needed some time out of the saddle.

"We'll stay here the night," Clint said. "Get something to eat, some sleep, let the horses rest."

"You mean let me rest," Willis said. "I'm holding you back."

"Nonsense," Clint said. "There's no need to push the horses. By the tracks I can see we're only a couple of days behind them."

"So if we push—"

"If we push it, you and your horse won't make it," Clint said. "And you have to make it, Lou. You represent the town."

They reined in their horses in front of a cantina and went inside.

THIRTY-ONE

They ate and drank well in the cantina, but discovered there was no hotel in the town. But they were able to bed down in the stable with their horses, as there were no other strangers in town.

They each made themselves a bed of hay in an empty stall.

"Comfortable?" Clint asked.

"More so than I was on the hard ground these past nights," Willis said.

"Well, don't get used to it," Clint said, reclining in his stall. "It'll be back to the hard ground tomorrow night."

"Hopefully I'll get a good night's sleep tonight, then."

"We both will," Clint said. "Tomorrow we'll be refreshed."

Willis ached from head to foot, and doubted he'd be

refreshed by morning. But maybe he wouldn't hurt so much by then. Fording the river had taken more out of him than even he thought.

In moments Clint heard Willis snoring. He hoped the night's sleep would help the man stand up to the rest of the trip. It was true he could have moved faster without him, and he didn't know how much help Willis would be in a gun battle, but he'd started to like the man. Leaving him behind, alone, didn't appeal to him. Though he could have left him right here in town and picked him up on the way back.

Maybe he'd make that very offer to the man in the morning.

Within moments, he was asleep as well.

In the morning they returned to the cantina for breakfast, and Clint made his offer.

"Why don't you stay here," he said.

"And do what?" Willis asked.

"Just wait," Clint said. "I'll pick you up on the way back."

"So then I can tell the mayor I went with you and helped you get the money back?" Willis asked. "That'd be a lie. I can't do that, Clint."

"I wouldn't think any less of you."

"I would think less of myself," Willis said. "No, I have to go with you."

"Suit yourself."

"If you tried to leave me behind," Willis told him, "I'd follow you."

"All right," Clint said. "We won't discuss it anymore."

"Fine."

They finished their breakfast and went to the stable to saddle their horses.

As they rode out of town, Willis realized he did feel somewhat better. His butt was getting used to the saddle, and his muscles didn't ache so much.

"So what are we going to do when we catch up to them?" he asked.

"I don't know yet," Clint said. "It'll depend on where we catch up to them, and how many of them there really are."

"So, in other words," Willis said, "we don't have a plan."

"No, Clint said, "we don't."

"And you've done this before?"

"Done what before exactly?"

"Hunted men with no plan as to how to capture them," Willis explained.

"Once or twice."

"And has it turned out all right for you?"

"Once or twice."

"Well, then," Willis said, "I can earn my keep on this ride."

"How?"

"I'm a lawyer," he said. "Making a plan is what I do."

"I see," Clint said, "so you'll come up with a plan to capture them?"

"Or kill them," Willis said. "I will."

Clint leaned over and clapped his hand on Willis's shoulder.

"If you do that," he said, "then you will have earned your keep."

"Then while we ride," Willis said, "I'll give it some thought. And by the time we catch up to them, I'll have a plan."

"I'll count on it," Clint said.

THIRTY-TWO

Jimmy McCall rode into Casa Madera, the new town the Donovan gang was going to hit, and saw that Donovan had been right. Just riding down the street, he saw several other gringos walking about. For this reason he did not attract that much attention as he rode in.

He saw that the town had two hotels, and a rather large jail. In addition, more than one cantina and several cafés. Finally, he saw the town's bank, an impressive adobe structure with bars on the windows. It looked more like a jail than the actual jailhouse did.

He stopped at the livery stable, arranged for his horse to be taken care of, then carried his rifle and saddlebags to the closest hotel.

The clerk handed him a key with a smile and said, "Enjoy your stay with us, *señor.*"

"Thanks," McCall said. "I will."

He went to his room, tossed his saddlebags onto the bed, and leaned his rifle in the corner. Then he walked to the window and looked down at the town's main street. This was a growing community, and would be a good haul for the Donovan gang.

But McCall was still upset about the last job they'd pulled, because people had been killed that day. When they'd hit the Windspring bank, McCall didn't see any reason for the killing. Booth had simply gunned down a teller for no reason, and Long reacted by shooting the bank manager. People who had their hands in the air and were not resisting at all.

When they got outside the bank, naturally the sheriff and deputy were there to greet them, so they had to be killed as well.

Now, more than ever, McCall wanted out. He wanted his money, and he wanted to go back to his kids. But he knew if he tried to leave now, Donovan would kill him. He could have ridden out now, and Donovan would come and find him and kill him. And if his kids were with him, Donovan would kill them, too.

So he had to do this last job, and get his money. If the gang members turned on each other, he'd have to try to come out in one piece and get away.

But that was for later. Right now he needed to go out, familiarize himself with the town, and with the bank, so he'd have all the information Donovan needed when he got there.

"What about help?" Willis asked Clint. "You know a lot of men who are good with guns. I mean, I assume that you do."

"I do," Clint said, "but it would take too long for them to get here."

"What about getting some men here?" Willis asked. "And deputizing them?"

"We're in Mexico, Lou," Clint said. "We don't have any authority here to deputize."

"Well, hell," Willis said, "how the hell can the two of us surround a whole gang?"

"I don't know," Clint said. "I thought it was your job to come up with a plan."

"Yeah, but—okay, I'll keep thinking about it," Willis said. "I guess I need to approach it more like a legal problem."

Clint didn't know how the lawyer intended to do that, but at least it would keep him busy.

They continued to ride, to follow the tracks left by the gang, who continued to skirt around towns and villages until they came to a small one called San Angel. Here, it looked as if the entire gang had simply ridden right into town.

"Let's see what they were up to here," Clint said as they rode in.

It only took minutes for Clint to discover there was no law in San Angel, and that it was more of a village than a town.

"With no law this would have been a perfect stop for them," he said.

The streets were empty as Clint and Willis walked their horses over to the cantina.

"Aren't too many places they could have gone here," Clint said. "I'll check in the cantina, you go over to that hotel."

"Okay. What do I do if I find them?"

"You won't find them," Clint assured him. "They've been here and they're gone. Just find out what you can about what they did while they were here, and where they might have gone."

"Okay."

Lou Willis left his horse and walked over to the hotel.

Clint went into the little cantina and walked up to the bar. There were a few men in the place, and one black-haired Mexican woman working the floor. Instead of the bartender approaching, the woman came over. She had seen better days, but they were far in her past. Up close he could see the lines of age on her face, and the sag to her body.

"I am Rosalita. Somethin' I can get for you, *señor?*" she asked, her hands on her hips. "Or do for you? Perhaps you are lonely?"

"I'm not lonely, thanks," Clint said. "I'd just like a *cerveza.*"

"Miguel!" she yelled. "*Cerveza* for the gringo!"

The bartender, a big guy in his thirties who scowled at Clint, came over with a beer and set it down.

"Anythin' else, *señor?*" she asked.

"I have a question or two."

"About what?"

"About a group of men who rode in here about two days ago," he said. "All gringos."

"*Sí,*" she said, "I remember them. One of them interrupted me and Rodrigo when we were, ah, how you say, doin' business?"

"He did, huh?" Clint asked. "Was he the leader? A big man?"

"*Sí.*"

"And this Rodrigo. Were they friends?"

"*Sí, señor.* When the gringos left, Rodrigo rode with them."

"Any idea where they were going?" Clint asked.

She shrugged.

"Rodrigo did not tell me."

"Were all the gringos in here?"

"*Sí, señor.*"

"Did they stay awhile?"

"No, they did not."

"So you did not have time to, uh, do business with any of them?"

"*No, señor,*" she said. "They ate, they drank, and they rode out."

"Interesting."

Rosalita put her hand on his arm and said, "If you want to do business while you are here, *señor*, you let me know."

"I will," Clint said, wondering if she was the only whore in the village. "Don't worry, I'll let you know."

She rubbed her hand up and down his arm, then moved away.

THIRTY-THREE

Across the street Willis found the desk clerk asleep with his head down.

"Excuse me," he said as he approached the desk.

The man didn't move. When he reached him, Willis didn't hear any breathing, and he wondered if the man had passed away.

"*Señor?*"

Excuse me?"

Nothing.

There was an open register book near the man. Willis reached out and slammed the book closed.

The clerk jerked his head up and stare wild-eyed at the lawyer.

"Oh, *señor!*" he said. "I was havin' a bad dream."

"Looked to me like you were sleeping pretty soundly," Willis said.

The clerk sat back and wiped his face with his hands.

He was in his fifties, a weathered-looking man with a bushy mustache.

"What can I do for you, *señor?*"

"I want to ask you some questions about a group of men who rode in here a couple of days ago."

"Ah, the gringo outlaws," the man said. "You are the law, chasing them perhaps?"

"I'm looking for them, yeah," Willis said. "Did they stay overnight?"

"No, *señor.* They went to the cantina, and then left town. But Rodrigo, he went with them."

"Rodrigo?"

"*Sí.* He came here about two days before them, stayed in one of our rooms, spent time with Rosalita. When the outlaws came, they went to his room and chased Rosalita out. She ran through the lobby naked, *señor.*" The man shuddered. "*Señor*, it was not a pretty sight. Rosalita is not a young girl anymore."

"I see."

"You should ask your questions at the cantina, *señor*," the clerk said.

"Yes, I will," Willis said. "Thank you."

"*De nada, señor.*"

Before Willis got through the door, the clerk's head was back on the desk, and he was asleep.

When Willis walked into the cantina, Clint waved at Miguel for two more beers. The big bartender had them on the bar when Willis reached it.

"Anything?" Clint asked.

Willis told Clint what the desk clerk had told him.

"That's pretty much what I found out here," Clint said.

Willis looked across the room at the woman, who was staring at him.

"Is that Rosalita?" he asked.

"It is."

"I can see what the clerk meant."

"Yeah."

"So what do we do now?" Willis asked. "We're not going to stay here, are we?"

They both looked across the cantina at Rosalita, and Clint said, "No, we'll move on, keep following the tracks. I was just hoping we'd have an idea where they were headed so we wouldn't just have to follow."

"What about food?" Willis asked.

They turned their back on Rosalita and leaned on the bar.

"We'll get some *enchiladas* to take with us," Clint said.

THIRTY-FOUR

Rodrigo was on watch, and Donovan came over and joined him. They were far enough away from camp where the other men couldn't hear them.

"Rodrigo, by now you've figured out what's goin' on, right?"

"Sí, señor," Rodrigo said. "Your men, they are going to turn on you."

"Yeah, but not 'til after this job," Donovan said. "Can I count on you when the time comes?"

"Sí, señor," Rodrigo said, "I am with you, but who else is with us? Even your *segundo*, Carter, is ready to kill you."

"That's what I thought," Donovan said. "We can count on Jimmy McCall."

"Are you sure, *señor?*" Rodrigo asked. "That man, I do not think he likes you so much."

"That's okay," Donovan said. "Jimmy's loyal. We go

back a long way. He don't have to like me to help keep me alive."

"If you say so, *señor*."

"Besides," Donovan said, "after he helps us kill the others, we'll kill him."

"And split the money two ways?"

"You bet."

Rodrigo looked at Donovan.

"*Señor*, you are not thinking perhaps you will kill me then and keep the money for yourself?"

"Rodrigo," Donovan said, as if taken aback, "we go back even further than me and Jimmy. Look, I've got to trust somebody, and that somebody is you."

"*Gracias, señor.*"

"And you gotta trust somebody," Donovan said, "and that's me, right?"

Rodrigo studied Donovan for a long moment, then said, "As you say, *señor*."

Donovan slapped Rodrigo on the back, then turned and looked over at the camp, where the men were sitting at the fire.

"I'll get somebody to relieve you in a few minutes," Donovan said. "I'll feel a lot safer if you're in camp with me."

"As you wish, *señor*," Rodrigo said. "You are *el jefe*."

"Yes, I am, Rodrigo," Donovan said. "I'm the *jefe*."

They were camped a few miles outside Casa Madera, where Jimmy McCall was still doing his reconnoitering.

Just outside of town was a mission, and McCall went there last. He walked into the church and sat in one of the pews, staring up at the crucifix above the altar.

He heard somebody behind him, turned, and saw a priest coming down the aisle toward him.

"Is there something I can do for you, my son?" the Mexican priest asked.

"I don't think so, *Padre*," McCall said. "I think I'm beyond your help."

"And God's help?"

"I'm beyond that, too."

"That cannot be, my son," the priest said. He had gray hair, but wasn't that old, maybe forty. He had his hands inside the sleeves of his robe. "None of us is beyond the help of God."

"I hope you're right, *Padre*," McCall said. "I got four kids countin' on me."

"Perhaps you should go to them."

"I wish I could, *Padre*," Jimmy said. "I just can't right now."

"Well, my son, I do not know everything that is weighing heavily upon you," the priest said, "but I am here if you need to talk further."

"Thank you, Father," Jimmy said. "I appreciate it."

"I am Father Francisco," the priest said. "I am always here."

McCall nodded, and Father Francisco withdrew.

Jimmy McCall was not a religious person. He had gone into the church simply to find a quiet place to sit, and think. He didn't think anyone—priest or no priest— could help him with this problem. He needed to get away from this gang, away from Andy Donovan, alive, with money, to go back to his kids. It seemed like a heavy task at the moment.

He left the church and headed back to town. He had spent the day scouting it thoroughly, and now it was time to take a look at what kind of law Casa Madera had to offer.

THIRTY-FIVE

Clint and Willis sat on the trail and ate their *enchiladas* and *frijoles refritos*.

"Are we camping here for the night?" Willis asked.

"I don't think so," Clint said. "We still have a few hours of daylight ahead. We might as well put them to good use."

Willis put the last of his *enchilada* into his mouth, then scooped up the rest of his beans.

"Well," he said, licking his fingers, "after that meal I'm ready to ride."

Clint finished his own food and stood up, brushing his hands together.

"Let's take the horses over there to that watering hole and let them drink," he said.

They grabbed the reins of their horses and walked them to the water. While the animals drank, they filled their canteens. As Clint was putting his back on his saddle, he saw the dust in the distance.

"We got company," Clint said.

"Who?" Willis looked around.

"I don't know, but there are a few of them," Clint said.

"The gang?"

"Only if they're coming back," Clint said. "Might just be some riders coming for water. Let's wait and see."

"Shouldn't we get out of here?" Willis said.

"Just stand fast, Lou," Clint said. "Don't panic. Let's see who it is."

As the riders came close, they were able to see the uniforms.

"Soldiers?" Willis asked.

"No," Clint said, *"Rurales."*

"Which are?"

"Local police," Clint said.

"That's good, right?"

"Depends on if they look at us," Clint said. Abruptly, he took the badge from his pocket and pinned it to his shirt. "Let's see if this helps."

"I hope it does," Willis said. "How many are there?"

"Looks like half a dozen."

"They'll respect the badge, right?"

"I don't know, Lou," Clint said. "I don't know."

As the riders came closer, they could hear the sounds of their swords clanking. They were armed with blades, pistols, and rifles, and several of the men wore bandoliers across their chest. Clint didn't want to tell Willis the truth, but many times the local *rurales* were made up of men who were at one time bandits. And some of them used their authority as a license to steal.

They let their horses drink as the *rurales* approached them.

"Señores," the leader said. He had two stripes, while all the rest had one. He was not an officer, or a sergeant, but he was in command there.

"Good afternoon."

"If you do not mind," he said, "we will water our horses with you."

"Not at all," Clint said. "It's more your water hole than it is ours. It's your country."

"Sí, señor," the man said, "it is." The man smiled, showing a mouthful of golden teeth. He said something in Spanish to his men, and they moved their horses to the water while they remained mounted. Clint didn't like that. It gave them an advantage, which they seemed anxious to keep.

He was ready.

THIRTY-SIX

The leader kept his eyes on Clint. It was either because of the badge, or because he instinctively knew that Clint was more of a danger than Willis.

Willis stood beside Clint, who could feel the man's nervousness. He just hoped the lawyer wouldn't do anything foolish. That ranged from going for his gun, to possibly running. Anything could have set off an already volatile situation.

"I see you are wearin' a badge, *señor*," the leader said.

"That's right, Corporal."

"Are you in my country in pursuit of someone?"

"We are."

"You understand that your badge gives you no authority here."

"I do understand that," Clint said. "Unfortunately, we had no choice but to follow the trail where it lead us."

"I understand."

Clint was looking at the boots the men were wearing. While they were in uniform, their boots were worn and did not seem to match.

While their horses drank, the mounted men watched Clint and Willis closely. The corporal was the only one who dismounted. He hooked his thumbs in his gun belt.

"How far are you going, *señor*?" the corporal asked.

"We don't know," Clint said. "As far as the tracks go, I guess."

"What direction are these tracks leading?"

"South, so far."

"Perhaps the men you seek are going to Mexico City?"

"Perhaps."

"Mexico City is a very expensive place," the man said. "Perhaps the men you are chasing are bank robbers?"

"I'm not at liberty to say," Clint replied.

"Perhaps you and your *compadre* have some money on you?" the corporal said. "There are, you know, travel taxes that must be paid."

"Taxes?" Willis asked.

"*Sí,*" the corporal said, "and we are authorized to collect them."

"I'm afraid I'm not authorized to pay them," Clint said.

"In that case," the man said, "I am afraid you cannot go any further."

"Is that right?"

"In fact," the corporal said, "you should not even be watering your horses."

"Too late," Clint said.

"Ah, well, if your horses have already drunk, and you have already filled your canteens, I am afraid we must insist on the taxes."

As if to back his words, several of his men put their hands on their guns.

"Corporal, I understand you have faith in numbers," Clint said, "but if any of your men go for their guns, you'll be the first one killed."

"*Señor*, as a lawman yourself, you would kill a member of the *rurales?*"

"I'm afraid I don't believe you and your men are *rurales*," Clint said. "I think you're bandits who happened to come across a group of *rurales*, killed them, and took their uniforms."

"You have proof of this, *señor?*"

"I'll bet if your men turned around, we'd see some bullet holes in the backs of those uniforms."

"*Señor . . .*" the corporal said warningly.

One of the mounted men made the mistake. He went for his gun, drawing a pistol from his bandolier. Clint drew quickly, shot the man from his saddle. A second man grabbed for his rifle, but Clint shot him as well.

Willis drew his gun from his holster, but wasn't sure what to do next. He looked to Clint, who was pointing his gun at the corporal.

The corporal, in turn, was holding his hands out to Clint, palms out.

"No, no, *señor*," he said, "there is no need for that." He waved an arm at his remaining men and said, *"Basta!"*

The remaining men took their hands from their guns. Clint looked down at the two fallen men. They had landed facedown, and he could see the bullet holes in the backs of their uniform shirts.

"*Señor*, you are very good with your gun," the corporal said. Not that he really was a corporal.

"He should be," Willis said. "His name is Clint Adams."

Clint could see by the look on the man's face that he recognized the name, but Willis didn't know that.

"He's the Gunsmith," Willis said.

"I recognized the name, *señor*," the man told Willis.

"You and your boys better be on your way," Clint said. "And pick up your dead."

"We want no trouble with you, *señor*," the man said. He spoke to his men in Spanish, and they dismounted, picked up the dead men, and draped them over their horses.

The man in the corporal's uniform mounted up and waited. When all the men were once again mounted, he looked at Clint.

"I suspect, *señor*, that you are looking for the seven or eight men we passed yesterday."

"That could be."

"Just to show you there are no hard feelings for you killing Julio and Cesare, I will tell you that they are camped outside a town called Casa Madera."

"How far is that?" Clint asked.

"One day's ride," the man said. "I suspect they have sent another man into town to scout ahead. That is what I would have done."

"What kind of town is Casa Madera?" Clint asked.

"A growing town, *señor*," the man said.

"And the bank?"

"Full."

Clint had the feeling these *bandidos* had probably considered robbing that bank themselves, but they were outnumbered by the Donovan gang. Maybe this gang wanted Clint and Willis to remove the Donovan gang from their path.

"Much obliged for the information," Clint said.

"De nada, señor. Buenas suerte."

Clint and Willis kept their guns in their hands until the gang of *bandidos* was out of sight.

"Jesus Christ," Willis said.

"Holster your gun, Willis."

"I'm sorry I didn't back you—"

"But you did," Clint said. "You drew your gun, you were ready. If there had been more shooting, you would have been there."

"I can't believe how quickly you shot those men out of their saddles."

"I had to make an impression so that there wouldn't be more shooting."

"Well, you did. How did you know they weren't real lawmen?"

"Their boots," Clint said. "They didn't go with the uniforms."

Clint and Willis backed their horses away from the water hole and mounted.

"You think they'll be waiting for us up ahead?"

"Maybe," Clint said, "but I have the feeling he told us about Donovan and his gang for his own reasons.

They probably want Donovan and his men out of the
way so they can rob the Casa Madera bank."

"So they'll be around waiting."

"I'm sure," Clint said. "But right now, we're going to
ride for Casa Madera and see if they were telling the
truth."

THIRTY-SEVEN

Jimmy McCall was sitting in the cantina, working on a bottle of tequila. It was time for somebody from the gang to come into town and get the information he'd collected. He doubted Donovan would come himself, and the *segundo* was no longer a trusted ally. For this reason McCall expected the Mexican, Rodrigo, to come in. So he wasn't surprised when the Mexican walked in.

"Hello, *amigo*," he said, sitting with McCall.

McCall had two glasses on the table. He pushed one at Rodrigo, who filled it himself from the bottle.

"*Gracias,*" he said, and downed it. "You were expecting me, eh?"

"I was."

"*Bueno,*" Rodrigo said. "*Señor* Donovan told me you were good. He told me you would not be surprised when I walked in."

"He knows me pretty well."

"That is also what he said," Rodrigo said, pouring himself another drink.

"Okay," McCall said, "let me give you the rundown here."

"Bueno," Rodrigo said, "that is what I am here for. The—how do you say?—rundown."

McCall told Rodrigo about the town first, then about the bank.

"They have two guards on the inside," he finished. "Both armed."

"No guards outside?"

"No," McCall said, "but they have a sheriff and two deputies."

"What are they like?"

"The sheriff is experienced," McCall said, "but the deputies are young. I don't think they'll be that much trouble."

"Very good."

"In fact," McCall said, "I think we can take care of them even before we go into the bank."

"How?"

McCall told him his plan.

"I will tell Donovan what you have said," Rodrigo said. "He will be pleased."

"I think so, too."

"How much attention have you attracted?"

"Not much," McCall said. "There are a lot of other gringos in town. I've played poker with some of them, so I've kind of started to blend in."

"That is good."

Rodrigo stood up. Nobody in the cantina was paying them any special attention.

"You better walk out alone," McCall said. "I'll just stay here awhile longer."

"I will see you soon," the Mexican said, and left.

McCall heard his horse as the man rode out of town. Then he stood up, went to the bar, got a beer, and carried it back to the table. He finished it with the rest of the tequila.

When Rodrigo reached the camp, he waved at Long, who was on watch, and rode in. Donovan waited for him to dismount.

"Did you see McCall?"

"*Sí, señor.*"

"And?"

"You were right," Rodrigo said. "He is very good at his job."

"Good," Donovan said. "Come over to the fire and tell me what he said. Every detail."

"*Sí, patron.*"

THIRTY-EIGHT

Clint and Willis looked down at the outlaw camp. There was a man on watch, but they had come from behind without being seen.

"Not much of a watchman if we were able to sneak up on them," Willis said.

"It's just a habit," Clint said. "I'm sure they're not expecting a posse at this point."

"Do you see your man?"

"Well, I've never seen McCall before, but I do have a description," Clint said. "I think I'd be able to spot him."

"From here?"

"He's got red hair."

"Ah," Willis said. "That would help."

As they watched, they counted. Both of them came to a total of seven men, but not one with red hair.

"Okay," Clint said, "this is gold."

"What is?"

"He's not there," Clint said. "That means he's in town, scouting."

"So we go to town?"

"And find him, and take him back home."

"What about Donovan and his gang?"

"Maybe McCall will help us catch them," Clint said. "But first we have to find him and talk to him."

"We have to get into that town without the gang seeing us."

"Right," Clint said. "We'll have to circle around and come into town from another direction."

"And hope the gang doesn't hit the bank while we're doing that."

"Right," Clint said, "so we better get moving."

Rodrigo finished telling Donovan about McCall's plan to get the lawmen out of the way before they hit the bank.

"I like it," Donovan said.

"I thought you would, *señor*," Rodrigo said. "It is a good plan, no?"

"It's a very good plan," Donovan said. "It's the reason I recruited Jimmy in the first place."

"But . . . you still intend to kill him?"

"At some point," Donovan said, "yeah, but that don't mean I'll be happy about it."

Clint and Willis rode to the east before turning and heading for the town of Casa Madera. They were relieved when they rode in and did not find a gun battle going on in front of the bank.

"Maybe they robbed it and they're gone," Willis said.

"I don't think so."

"Why not?"

"No gunfire."

"How do you know?"

"I'd be able to smell it in the air."

As they rode down the street, they passed hotels, cantinas, a mercantile, a hardware store, a dress shop, and more small stores in new buildings.

"This is a growing town," Willis said. "The bank would be ripe."

"And we have to make sure it doesn't get plucked."

"So where to first? The sheriff?" Willis asked.

"As much as I'd like a beer first, yeah, the sheriff," Clint said.

"Well, a beer wouldn't be too bad," Willis observed.

Clint looked at him, then said, "Yeah, okay, a beer first."

THIRTY-NINE

Clint and Willis entered the cantina and ordered two beers. The place was new, with a shiny oak bar with gold trim.

"Not many towns like this in Mexico," Clint said. "Not yet anyway."

They looked around, saw a few men sitting at tables, nursing drinks. Then Clint's eyes fell on one of them in particular. He nudged Willis.

"What?"

Clint jerked his chin, and Willis looked. He saw a man, a gringo sitting at a table by himself with a beer mug and a bottle of tequila.

And he had red hair.

"Jesus," he said, "what a coincidence, huh?"

"I don't know, Lou," Clint said. "Let's find out."

They carried their beers to the man's table and looked down at him. Eventually the man raised his head and stared back.

"What?" he said.

"Jimmy McCall?"

"Who wants to know?"

"Your kids sent me."

"What do you know about my kids?" McCall demanded.

"I know they miss you," Clint said, "and they need you."

"Who are you?"

"My name is Clint Adams," Clint said. "This is Lou Willis. He's from the town of Windspring. You remember that town?"

McCall lowered his eyes, and his head. "I—I remember."

He was ashamed. Clint found that encouraging.

"Can we sit?"

"Sure," McCall said. "Why not?"

Clint and Willis pulled up chairs.

"Did you really see my kids?" McCall asked.

"I did."

"How are they?"

"Jason is doing the best he can," Clint said. "So is Jenny. But they need you."

"I know," McCall said. "I'm tryin' to get back to them."

"By riding with Donovan?"

McCall looked at Clint.

"You pretty much know everythin', huh?"

"I know you're in this town to scout the bank," Clint said. "I know the gang is camped just south of here. And I know if you leave with us now and go back to your kids, you could save yourself a lot of trouble."

"If I try to leave, Donovan will kill me."

"I'll make sure you get home safely," Clint said. "I promised that to your kids."

"But Donovan would come there lookin' for me," McCall said. "My kids could get hurt."

He had a point.

"Besides," McCall added, "I was in Windspring, part of that job. People died. I'd have to pay for that."

"Did you kill anyone?"

"No," McCall said, "I just scouted the job."

"Then I think if we could return the money, there'd be no need to turn you in." Clint looked at the lawyer. "What about it?"

"I think I can get the mayor to agree to that," Willis said.

"What do you say?" Clint asked.

"They're comin' in today," McCall said. "Seven of 'em."

"What are they waiting for?" Clint asked.

"I'm supposed to get the law out of the way."

"What is the law here?" Clint asked. "How many?"

"Sheriff, two deputies."

"Experienced?"

"The sheriff, yeah, but the two deputies look wet behind the ears."

Clint took a moment to consider the situation.

"We can't just ride out without warning the bank," McCall said.

"No," Clint said, "we have to do more than warn them. We'll have to help them."

"How?" Willis asked.

"We'll talk to the law," Clint said. "Set something

up. The gang may have more men, but if we're ready for them, that might even the odds."

"What if the sheriff don't believe us?" McCall asked.

"We'll make him believe us," Clint said. "Where's the harm in being ready?"

"We'd better do it soon, then," McCall said.

"You're willing?" Clint asked.

"If it'll get me out from underneath Donovan, yeah. Even though I'll have to go home without the money I came for."

Clint decided to address that problem when the time came.

FORTY

The three of them walked to the sheriff's office, where they found the lawman seated behind a large desk. The building was new, still smelled of fresh-cut wood. The usual potbelly stove had been replaced here by a newer-looking stove, good for cooking as well as heat. There was a pot of coffee on it. No deputies in sight.

"Sheriff," Clint said.

"Can I help you, boys?" the lawman asked.

"Nice setup you got here." Plenty of rifles on a locked rack, clean floor even back in the cell block.

"After some of the offices I've worked in . . ." the lawman said with a chuckle.

"Been at it a long time, have you?" Clint asked.

"The law? More than twenty years."

"Then you must be used to trusting your instincts."

"I am," the sheriff said. "And my instincts are tellin' me now that you're leadin' up to somethin'."

"My name's Clint Adams, Sheriff," he said, "and I have a story to tell you . . ."

To his credit, the sheriff—whose name was Latham—listened quietly, did not ask any questions until Clint was finished.

The lawman looked directly at Jimmy McCall and said, "Are you sure you want to do this?"

"Yes, sir."

"When are they comin' in?"

"It should be today," McCall said.

"Minutes? Hours?"

"Hours," Jimmy said. "They're waitin' for me to . . . to take care of you and your deputies."

"Then we better get movin'," Latham said. He stood up, grabbed his hat, and jammed it on his head. "I'll need to find my deputies, and talk to the bank manager. Mr. Adams, you have any suggestions?"

"I think the most experienced of us should be on the outside, Sheriff," Clint said. "We can put Willis here and your deputies inside."

"Makes sense," Latham said. "You think of anythin' else, just let me know. I'm open to any other suggestions."

"Good to know, Sheriff," Clint said.

They followed the lawman out.

Donovan looked up at the position of the sun, then waved Carter over to where he and Rodrigo were seated.

"Get the men mounted," he said. "Time to go in."

"How we gonna play it?" Carter asked.

"Same as last time," Donovan said.

"Last time we stayed in town awhile."

"Well, this time we're gonna ride directly up to the bank," Donovan said. "From that point on, it'll be the same. Except I want Booth on the outside, with the horses. We don't need him killin' somebody for no reason again."

"Right."

Carter walked over to the men, spoke briefly, and then they all started saddling their horses, happy that there was going to be some action.

"You ready?" Donovan asked Rodrigo.

"I am ready for anythin', *señor*."

"Yeah, me, too," Donovan said. "Let's get our horses saddled."

"*Señor*," Rodrigo asked, "you want me inside or out?"

"Inside," Donovan said, "and if any of these idiots looks ready to kill a teller, you kill them. Got it?"

"I got it, *señor*."

They managed to round up both deputies, and Latham introduced them to Clint, Willis, and McCall. He did not mention to them that McCall was formerly part of the gang. It wouldn't have mattered, though. Both young men were thrilled to meet the Gunsmith, and that was all they were concerned with.

"You boys will be inside the bank with the guards," Latham said, "and Mr. Willis here."

"Aw, Sheriff," one deputy said, "why can't we be outside?"

"I need you boys inside to make sure the people are safe," Latham said. "Understand? Their lives will be in your hands."

"Okay," one deputy said.

"Yes, sir," the other agreed.

"All right. Let's get into position. I'll come inside long enough to talk to Mr. Britton, the manager."

They headed for the bank. Clint and McCall were going to take up a position outside, soon to be joined by Latham.

"Sheriff?" Clint said as they approached the bank building.

"Yeah?"

"On their last job, some tellers got shot," Clint said. "I think some of Donovan's men are jumpy."

"What are you suggestin'?"

"I think we should stop them before any of them go into the bank."

"You might have a point," the lawman said. "I'll station the deputies and the guards by the windows. "When the shootin' starts, they can join in from there."

"Good idea."

"Appreciate your help on this, Adams."

"I'm just hoping we can get this done with no fatalities."

"Except for the bank robbers."

"Yes," Clint said, "except for them."

It would work to Jimmy McCall's benefit if Donovan were to catch a bullet and be killed. Then he wouldn't have to worry about the man coming for him, maybe even after a stint in jail.

Clint looked at McCall, figured he was thinking the same thing.

"Come in," he said to Jimmy, "let's get into position."

FORTY-ONE

Donovan stopped his men just outside of town. The street ahead of them was empty.

"What's the matter?" Carter asked.

"The street's too empty for a town this size."

"We are in Mexico, *señor*," Rodrigo said. "Siesta."

Donovan thought a moment, then said, "Yeah, okay," and started forward again.

Clint saw the gang stop at the head of the street and suddenly knew why. The damn street was too empty, but the sheriff had not wanted to take a chance that any civilians would be hurt. Clint couldn't blame him for that, but if Donovan changed his plans and the gang turned around, they'd be tracking and chasing them again.

After a few tense moments, however, the gang started forward again.

This was going to happen.

                      *   *   *

Jimmy McCall was nervous. Throwing in with Clint
Adams against Donovan's gang may not have been the
smart thing to do, but it seemed the only thing to do.
After all, his kids had sent Adams to find him, and to
help him. But if this didn't work, he could end up dead,
and then what would happen to his kids?

But it was too late to turn back now.

Lou Willis's heart was pounding as he stared out the
window of the bank. He could see Clint across the
street, as well as the sun glinting off the sheriff's badge.
He didn't know where McCall was. Hopefully, the man
wouldn't change sides again.

Behind him the bank tellers and clerks were all quiet
and nervous. That included the bank manager. But the
sheriff had agreed with Clint to brace the gang outside,
so there was no chance they'd get inside and put these
people at risk.

The two guards at the other window were older, experienced men. The deputies were sharing a window with
him, and the young men seemed as nervous as he was.
He only hoped that they—and he—would acquit themselves well.

Donovan led the gang right up to the front of the bank.
They remained mounted while he looked around.
At the slightest hint of something not right, he would
turn and ride out. But he glanced around only in passing because he was impressed by the size of the bank.
This would be a bigger haul than the bank in Windspring.

He looked around at his men, and then nodded.
They began to dismount.

Clint's last suggestion to Sheriff Latham was that they
wait until the gang was in the act of dismounting. The
sheriff agreed. The gang would be off balance with one
foot still in the stirrup.

As the gang began their dismount, the sheriff stepped
out into the open and shouted, "Hold it right there!"

Donovan froze—as Clint had hoped—with one foot still
in his stirrup. He looked across the street, saw the man
with the badge, then saw two other men step out into
the open—and one of them was Jimmy McCall.

They'd been had!

He went for his gun and shouted, "Have at it, men!"

As the gang drew, Clint, McCall, and Latham began to
fire. Two men who had remained in the saddle—
probably to watch the horses—were the first to be hit.
The bullets took them from their saddles and dumped
them on the ground.

From behind the gang came the sound of shatter-
ing glass as the guards and deputies broke the windows and began to fire. They now had the gang in a
cross fire.

Donovan knew they were done. His only hope was
to try to get away. The gang's horses were scattering,
frightened by all the gunfire. He grabbed his, though,
because the saddlebags held the money they'd stolen
so far.

Rodrigo had the same idea. He grabbed his horse and tried to remount. The two men thought to ride out of town amid the action.

Jimmy McCall saw Donovan remount and knew what the man was going to try.

"Donovan!" he shouted, and moved farther out into the street.

Clint knew what McCall was doing. He wanted a clean shot at Donovan, but he was also opening himself up to gunfire from other members of the gang. Clint stepped out to cover the man's back while he took his shot at Donovan. He had to kill three gang members who were drawing a bead on McCall, but Jimmy got his shot off.

Donovan felt the bullet strike him in the back, between his shoulder blades. It knocked the wind out of him, but he thought he would be able to stay in the saddle, right up until the time he felt the ground come up and strike him in the face.

Rodrigo saw Donovan fall, knew the other members of the gang were done, but he continued to ride, and was the only member of the gang to escape.

McCall scrambled and caught Donovan's horse before the animal could run off. He led it back to the bank, where Willis and the others had come out.

"Mr. Willis," McCall said.

Willis turned.

McCall reached into one of the saddlebags and brought out a fistful of money.

"It's all here, sir," McCall said. "Your bank's money."

"Thank you, Mr. McCall," Willis said. Then he looked at Clint. "Thank you."

FORTY-TWO

The door to the house opened, and all four kids stepped out. Jason and Jenny each held their brother and sister, Jesse and Simon. But when the children saw their father dismounting, they all ran to him.

Clint watched as the four children inundated their father, dragging him to the ground with the force of their hugs. He dismounted himself and simply watched the family reunion.

"Are you back to stay, Pa?" Simon asked.

"I'm back to stay, squirt."

"Really, really?" Jesse asked.

"Yes, sprite," McCall said, "really, really."

McCall got to his feet, put one hand on Jason's shoulder, and the other on Jenny's.

"Mr. Adams told me how responsible you two have been," he said. "I'm real proud of you."

"You're not gonna have to go off again, Pa, are you?" Jason asked hopefully. "I mean, for a job or somethin'?"

"No, son," McCall said. "We should be okay for a while—thanks to Mr. Adams. I think from this point on, you can go back to bein' a kid. I'll be the pa."

And, Clint thought, thanks to the reward the Windspring bank had paid him. Clint and Willis had both hidden the fact that McCall was part of the gang, and Willis arranged for the reward. It was more money than the family had ever seen before, more than McCall could make in two years of working at a steady job—if he could even find one.

Jesse walked over to Clint and yanked on his arm. When he looked down, she crooked her little finger at him. He bent down.

"Thank you," she said. She threw her little arms around his neck and kissed him soundly on the cheek.

Jenny ran to Clint and also hugged and kissed him firmly.

"I'm gonna make a big welcome home supper," she said. "Will you stay and eat with us?"

Clint looked over at the others, and they all seemed to be watching him expectantly.

"That'd be real nice, Clint," McCall said.

Clint looked back at Jenny and said, "That sounds like an offer I just can't refuse, Jenny."

Watch for

TICKET TO YUMA

373rd novel in the exciting GUNSMITH series
from Jove

Coming in January!

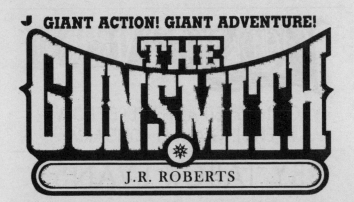

GIANT ACTION! GIANT ADVENTURE!

THE GUNSMITH

J.R. ROBERTS

penguin.com/actionwesterns

M455AS0812

GIANT-SIZED ADVENTURE FROM AVENGING ANGEL LONGARM.

BY TABOR EVANS

penguin.com/actionwesterns

M456AS0812